THE *Love* YOU KNOW

—

By Elaina Lyons

ISBN 979-8-218-13501-0

————

*For the ones who broke my heart
and the ones who put it back together.*

————

CHAPTER

ONE

—

LYING ON MY STOMACH, I FELT HIS fingers reach under my shirt and begin to trace the curves of my back, slowly. They seemed to linger at each point, circling little curlicues of motion before gently moving upward. I closed my eyes. Everything about the moment was perfect. I could feel myself breathing slower and slower, abandoning myself to the softness of his hands. Neither of us said anything. Neither of us needed to. The room was dark and quiet, with only occasional staticky transmissions from dispatch calling other stations to action. But not ours. Everyone was asleep, presumably, but being together like this was dangerous nonetheless. It was a calculated risk we took every shift. The couch creaked a little underneath me as I shifted my weight and put my head on my hands to look at him. He was sitting beside me on the floor, one arm still under my shirt. I could feel his hands twist the clasp of my bra just slightly as if he was going to try to take it off, but I knew he wasn't. Not out there. There were places for that in the station but the downstairs lounge, a few steps from the bunk room, certainly wasn't one of them. His little hand motion, the tenderness with which he pretended to wrestle with the hooks, made me crave him even more.

"What is it?" he asked.

His eyes were so gentle and kind. When I was with him, I felt like he saw me and no one else. When I was with him, I knew I saw him and no one else.

"What did you think when you first saw me?" I whispered.

He smiled a little, playfully, and took his hand out, resting it on my back.

"I thought you had really pretty eyes and a very, very strong personality. And I thought I wanted to get to know you more."

I looked at him, studying everything from the five o' clock shadow on his cheeks to the mildly thinning brown hair that peaked out of his baseball cap. He tilted his head to the side a bit, nodding as if to ask me to answer my own question.

"I don't know," I lied, thinking back to January when I first saw him walk through the bay doors. Three months had gone by so quickly, and yet it felt like so very long since that first moment. "I guess I thought you were, sort of mysterious in a way."

He laughed.

"What's mysterious about this?" he said, making a circle around his face with one finger. "There's not a single thing mysterious about me."

"Well I know that now. But I didn't then. I mean, not mysterious like 'oh god, he's so strange, I must know who this man is' sort of a way. But more like, I was intrigued. I was curious."

"Mhmm. Whatever you say."

"I'm being serious! Oh, whatever."

"Let's go somewhere."

"Where? Like upstairs?"

"No. Let's go on a trip. Just you and me."

I looked at him to try to gauge whether he was joking. It was usually easy to tell – his eyes would sparkle a little bit and one side of his mouth would curve into a tentative smile. But sometimes, occasionally, it wasn't so easy to figure him out.

"Oh ha-ha. Not funny."

"I'm being serious."

"Parker," I said, sitting up. "How would that possibly happen?"

"I don't know. But is it wrong to think about it?"

Probably, I thought. *But not more wrong than any of this. Think away, Parker.*

"Kiss me?"

I smiled and leaned into him.

"Ambulance," he said.

"What?"

"Ambulance," he repeated, scrambling to his feet and rushing back to the bunk room. Through the double doors, I saw Rommie and Dawson sprint out to the bay and hop into the ambulance. It was always like this. Scattered times throughout the day, 15 minutes if we were lucky, every third day. We had 24 hours at a time around each other, but only a sprinkling of minutes really *with* one another. I lay on the couch, staring into the empty fireplace. We'd had a fire going a few hours before but it had long since burned itself out. I hadn't noticed it when Parker was there but, without him, I realized just how chilly the room was.

Parker was probably going to go to bed, but I didn't see a point. I'd have to be up in a couple hours anyway. I grabbed my phone.

"Parker," I sent.

Typing…typing…typing.

"Lucy."

He always called me Lucy. It started when he found out my full name. At the station, I'd always been Carrigan, which is what he called me until his third shift after he transferred in. I had asked him to look at my timesheet and, when he pulled it up, he apparently saw my entire name for the first time.

"Odette Lucille Carrigan.," he announced. Of course, he pronounced it "oh-ditty." "Where does that name come from?"

"It's pronounced *oh-det*. And my mom was really into Swan Lake."

"I think I'll call you Lucy." And ever since then, it'd been Lucy – but only to him.

"Tomorrow. Just a few minutes after shift," I typed. "We can just sit in a parking lot somewhere. Just be away from everything for a bit. Please."

Typing…typing…typing.
Pause.
Typing…typing…typing.
I knew the answer. I just had to ask anyway.
"I can't."

He didn't give an explanation, but I didn't need one. The idea of a trip away was something he could discuss because it was gloriously impossible. But a morning rendezvous meant more careful planning, simply because it was spontaneous. Somewhere far away, we could be other people. Here, we were us, and everyone knew us. Whoever said news travels fast in a small town hasn't been a part of the fire department. Everyone knows everything. Sometimes we snuck away. Sometimes we met for donuts or coffee or something else. Always somewhere hidden; always just us two. But I knew not to ask twice. If he said no, he meant no.

I felt my phone vibrate as I put it in my pocket. An unopened message from Avery. I turned the phone off and let it drop on my chest. The ceiling was old, each panel more stained than the last. I'd stared at that same ceiling for the last five years, in one part of the building or another. It was a wonder I hadn't fully memorized the water damage and miscolored tiles. I let my eyes lose their focus as they moved from one mark to the next. I don't know when I fell asleep, but I woke up to my alarm at 5:10. The sound of feet shuffling in the bay and voices greeting each other roused me out of my grogginess, at least a little bit.

"Slept on the couch last night?" Rommie asked, walking out of the bunk room, his duffel bag slung over his shoulder.

"Yeah, I was watching a movie. Must've fallen asleep."

"Well see ya next time."

I put my hand up in a half-wave/half-salute as I lifted myself into a seated position.

"See ya Rommie."

When I walked out to the bay, Parker's gear had already been replaced on the engine. *Till next time*, I thought. I put my gear away and went to the locker room to grab my keys and wallet, passing his on my way to mine. The door was slightly open, and as I looked away, I caught a glimpse of a picture of him and his wife taped to the inside of the door. They were sitting on what looked like a front stoop, him on the step above, her right below. His hand was on her shoulder, posed and perfect. They were both smiling. I turned quickly, made it to my locker, and grabbed my things before quickly leaving. Shift was over. Time to go home.

———

"How well do you think you communicate your needs?"

I played with my necklace, a silver chain with a "G" letter charm. My sister, Bridgett, had gotten it for me years before and I wore it every single day without fail. It was a gentle, albeit painful, reminder.

Not at all, I wanted to say. But I didn't. I took the cop out.

"I think I can probably work on it."

That's an understatement. Communication? What's that? We never talk. We never touch. What communication?

Dr. Forner looked in Avery's direction. Our counselor was short and balding, but he looked at least 10 years younger than he actually was. His face was bright and vibrant and his eyes were always energetic. Every session with him was like jump rope on a playground with a toddler. The endless energy was eternally exhausting. We were sitting – physically -- but mentally, emotionally, we never stopped jumping.

"Avery, you look like you have something to add. What's going through your mind right now?"

Avery didn't hesitate. It was like he'd been sitting on an answer even before I spoke.

"I think…I don't think we communicate at all. We barely talk. She's at work all the time," his voice sounded tired, but rushed, like he was trying to get the words out before someone made him stop. Maybe he thought that person would be me.

I looked at him sharply, hoping my eyes conveyed what I was thinking.

"I've been working a lot, too," he added.

Message received.

He always found a way to make it about me. It was always my fault. He worked worse hours than I did. I was gone every third day. He was gone almost all day every day. But work wasn't the real problem, was it? The issue isn't ever what you think it is. It's always deeper. There's always more.

"I asked to do this because she wouldn't. We do nothing together. We're barely married. I wear this fucking ring, and for what? For what?" He breathed loudly and spun the ring around his finger over and over again. I hadn't noticed until then just how loose it was. *Had it always been that loose?* I swallowed. Avery didn't show any emotion, outwardly. How he sounded and how he looked were entirely in opposition with one another. He just stared straight ahead, his eyes fixed on the blue clock on the wall next to Dr. Forner's head. It was such an odd juxtaposition in front of me – he had said his piece so incredibly angrily, but his face was entirely blank. Avery was so unpredictable when it came to any sort of demonstrative emotion. You could *hear* his anger or hurt or happiness or relief, but you could rarely see it. And then, very occasionally, his face would be so expressive you would think you could feel the world through his countenance. In all our time together, I had never cracked the code, so to speak. He was a persistent mystery.

"I can sense your anger, Avery. Now try saying that *to* Odette, instead of to me."

He just said it. Why are you making him repeat it?

Avery turned to look at me, as if on cue.

I hadn't looked him in the eyes in so long. I had forgotten what it felt like to feel them meet mine. The man who had been a stranger for so long became my husband again, just for a second. And then it faded. So, so quickly.

"I don't think we have anything in common anymore. I think whatever we had was gone a long time ago."

I didn't give myself time to process what he said before responding.

"Do you even want this to work?"

Funny of me, of all people, to ask that. Did I even want it to work?

Nothing.

Nothing.

Nothing.

Say something.

In the movies, the love of your life fights for you. They show some insanely spectacular display of affection and remorse and vow to do things differently. They stock your house full of your favorite flowers (white roses, in my case) and leave notes everywhere leading you to where they are, standing in some location significant to your relationship, like the café where you first met, or the sunflower field where they proposed, and they get down on one knee and ask you all over again to be theirs. And you say yes because you can feel they mean it this time. But in real life — in real life, there's no fight. There's no choosing you. There's just two people giving up because fighting for something you once had is just too damn hard, and the reward isn't quite enticing enough. Real life is resignation. And that's what I saw in Avery's eyes. I wondered if that's what he saw in mine.

"Avery, what are your thoughts right now?" Dr. Forner asked.

"I don't think we're us anymore. I think both of us have changed a lot in the last 8 years. A lot has happened. We don't see each other a lot because of my work and her work. It's hard to plan time to see each other. There's a lot of things here that I don't know if I can get past. And maybe she – you – can't. I don't know."

I wiped two rebel tears from my cheeks and grabbed a tissue from the side table.

"But I do want to try," he finished, rubbing his eyebrows like he was trying to force the thoughts back into his mind.

What does that even mean?

I felt like Dr. Forner read my mind.

"What does trying look like for you, Avery? And for you, Odette? Avery, you can go first."

"I honestly don't know." Avery looked down at his flannel button down and fiddled with a runaway string.

"Alright, that's OK," Dr. Forner said. "Odette?"

I looked at Dr. Forner, simply to avoid looking at Avery.

"I don't know. I don't know if it'll make much of a difference now. I don't think we have anything left."

"I understand what you're saying, Odette. But you two came to counseling for a reason. If you didn't want to work on your marriage, you wouldn't be here. If both of you are ready to end your marriage, there's nothing stopping you. But if you want to save it, you both have to commit to work at it – to come here every week and meet one another where you are. Is that something you're both willing to do?"

I leaned back in the couch and, for the first time throughout the entire session, noticed how far apart the two of us were sitting. Avery on one end, me on the other, leaning away from each other like strangers riding the Subway. The truth was, counseling had been his idea. Back months ago when things had reached a fever pitch. When I said I wanted to try for a baby and he said no without an explanation, as if I needed one – I knew why -- and we'd both gone totally mute. He slept on the couch – when that happened, I have no idea. One day I realized it'd been weeks since we'd slept in the same bed. But I couldn't even venture a guess when it started. And then one day, long after I'd completely given up trying, he asked me to make an appointment for us with a counselor. And I did. But I didn't know why he wanted to come here at all if he was so adamant about giving up. Maybe he needed someone else in order to tell me. Maybe he couldn't do it alone. There's power in numbers, right?

"I'd like to try," Avery said, looking at Dr. Forner.

Whether he actually did was a mystery to me. His voice sounded so resolved and so tired at the same time. We were both tired. But I couldn't be the one to say no. I couldn't be the one to end it. If he wanted to try, I had to be willing to do what the therapist suggested – meet him where he was.

"I am too."

"I'm glad to hear that. We're out of time for today but I want you to focus on a few things this week."

He started listing our assignments but I couldn't pay attention.

All I could think about was the gap between Avery and I on that couch, and the long, long road ahead that I wasn't even sure I wanted to go down.

CHAPTER
TWO

———

P ASSWORDS ARE FUNNY. NOT IN THE HA-HA meaning of the word – No, I mean their use is ironic. You forget them so easily and yet they're so important. I can't remember the number of times I've had to reset my bank passcode, simply because I consistently neglect to write it down. But when it came to other passwords, ones that I needed now for privacy's sake, ones that I needed to hide not from strangers but the people closest to me – those I never forgot. You learn all the tricks. All the apps. All the security features. You download the encrypted messengers and disable on-screen text notifications. You change their name in your phone just for added security. And, just to be 100 percent sure, you delete your conversations at the end of every day. At least, Parker told me to. That was his biggest sticking point. Every shift he asked if I'd deleted the messages. Every shift I said I had. But I hadn't. I never did. I couldn't bring myself to. Those messages were the one strand of proof I had that he was, in some way, mine. And I needed that proof. To the world, we were nothing. When those messages were gone, so were we. There had to be some evidence in the universe that he felt something for me – that we were more than just colleagues or friends. We couldn't have pictures together or cute statuses on Facebook declaring our anniversaries. We didn't get anniversaries. You always dream of your perfect fairy tale love story. We weren't a fairy tale. We weren't a story. We were the thoughts that the writer had while penning his grand masterpiece – the ones never brought to life on paper. We were invisible. Those messages made us real, or at least as real as we could be.

I'd learned over the last few months to keep my phone hidden. And I'd learned to be mindful of those handy passwords. I kept the phone on vibrate and checked every few minutes to make sure I hadn't missed anything. We never texted anyway, but occasionally he'd send me something on Instagram or one of the protected apps we used and I never wanted to miss it, regardless of how rare those messages were. So I checked religiously.

I was sitting at the kitchen table, doing some of that mindless checking, when I heard Avery clear his throat.

"I was thinking I could take Friday off. Maybe we could go to that new Italian place that just opened up. Trevor said it's really good."

He was standing over the sink, peeling an orange into about thirty different pieces. He'd just finished off a tin of leftover pasta from Olive Garden, where he'd gone with a friend, so he said, a few nights before. His eating habits never ceased to surprise me. I always made dinner on non-station days, and he always had take-out when I was gone. He'd never learned to cook and, in the seven years we'd been married, and eight we'd been together, he'd never once made me a meal. Until recently, I'd never really cared about it – I genuinely loved cooking – but lately I'd gotten sick of always being the one to figure everything out. Always being the one to pay the bills and take the dogs to the vet and make the meals and send gifts to his family on holidays. Sometimes I wanted him to do a little work. For months, perhaps years, it'd felt like our relationship was like a houseplant, but I was the only one watering it. And one day, maybe the day I met Parker, I stopped. And now we were here.

Avery's invitation seemed like his way of saying he was trying. He wanted to make an effort.

"Sure. I'm off that day. That's fine."

He stuffed the last of the orange in his mouth and nodded. A little bit of juice dripped down his beard and he wiped it quickly with the back of his hand. I loved that beard, or I used to. It was the first thing I'd noticed about him when we met. That felt like so long ago now. What a cliché we'd become. The once-in-love married couple that could barely stand each other anymore. What happened to us? There was a little bit of grey in his dark brown beard now. His father had gone gray early and Avery said he'd never end up like his father. I guess in a way, he already had.

He washed his hands quickly and walked over to me. I closed my eyes as he put his arms on my shoulders and rested his head on the top of mine. It felt crazy to me that someone so close to me could feel so incredibly foreign. Touch for us was abnormal. It just wasn't done. His sudden show of physical affection was odd and a little unnerving to say the least.

"I'll be back in a few hours."

I looked up at him as if to say I understood. I didn't ask where he was going and he didn't tell me. We were well past the point of checking in on each other's personal lives. There had been a time *we'd been* each other's personal lives. But now, there was an "us" and a "him and me" and they were entirely separate. I didn't know for sure he was seeing someone else. At least not currently. But I knew he had and truthfully, I didn't really care if it had started up again. It was 7 p.m. on a Wednesday and he was going out "for a few hours." Where else would he be going? But did it matter? Avery looked at me and smiled as he closed the front door behind him. I smiled back. I still loved his smile. I wondered if she, whoever she was, loved it too.

Maybe he was seeing someone else, maybe he wasn't. Maybe "Trevor" was really some woman he found on the internet and not a coworker I'd never met before. Maybe I thought he was cheating just so I felt better about doing it myself. Maybe guilt is easier swallowed when shared. Life is full of maybes.

It's funny trying to save something when you're actively killing it. It's like putting a dressing on a bleeding gash and not applying any pressure. Ostensibly, you're making an effort. But in reality, you're not doing a single thing to stop the bleeding. You're making a point, not an attempt. There we were, Avery and I, watching ourselves bleed and just opening the wound up some more, little by little, every day, all while confidently declaring we were "working on it."

My phone vibrated in my pocket and I pulled it out, half-hoping it would be a message from Parker.

"Thinking about you today, Odette. XOXO."

It was from Bridgett.

Just one year, I wished she'd forget. Or if she didn't, just not mention it.

March 9ᵗʰ. March 9ᵗʰ. March 9ᵗʰ.

I could remember when that date was filled with such hope

and longing and joy and all the best things.

Every year, I wished I could skip March altogether. And every year, I felt like shit for wanting to. For not wanting to do something sentimental and meaningful to remember, as if I needed some sort of ceremonial act to show I hadn't forgotten.

I got up and walked over to the kitchen. The orange peel was still in the sink, little pieces littering the sides and basin. What a little thing to get upset about. I wanted so badly to text Avery and bitch about it.

Couldn't have cleaned up your mess before you left?

Forget something on your way out?

But I didn't. Sometimes I wondered which was worse, arguing or staying silent to keep the peace. What peace can there be if you're never really honest? I wasn't angry about the orange. Who gets angry about an orange? I was angry about a shit load of things, but the orange was the one thing staring at me in that moment. That's how anger works, you know. It's never the tipping point that's the gigantic backbreaker of a problem. It's a million things that chip away one by one, and the thing that "causes" the huge explosion is just the thing that happens to be most visible at the time. I grabbed a paper towel and wiped out the peels, carefully grabbing each piece until they were all gone. One piece at a time.

I leaned on the counter and wrapped my thumb around my necklace. I was barely moving but I felt like I had no air left in my lungs. I took a gulp of air and exhaled slowly.

Shit.

Shit.

Shit.

March 9th.

Trying to ignore trauma, oddly enough, is like pretending to love someone. You can fool everyone else, but you can never really fool yourself.

It would've been my due date, March 9th. It should've been. So much time had passed. Sometimes, even when I concentrated hard, I couldn't remember how her little kicks felt in my belly, or the way her heartbeat sounded on each sonogram. I wanted to believe it was the years that eroded my memory, but I couldn't blame time. A part of me wanted to forget. That selfish, broken part of me that would rather be a childless woman by choice than the mother of a dead child. I wondered if Avery remembered. I reached into my pocket and typed a message to Parker.

"I miss you."

I didn't send it. I just stared at the little blinking line urging me to write more and clicked off my screen. There wasn't any more to say.

◆ ◆ ◆

Avery and I arrived at the restaurant at 6:30 on Friday. It was small and cozy and looked like it'd been around for much longer than a year. The ambiance was so well-established, like an old pizzeria that had been a town staple for two decades at least. To us, any business less than two years old was "new." What we meant was "new to us." We were led hastily to our seat by a pretty young woman with bright blue hair and long dangling dreamcatcher earrings.

"I'll be your waitress tonight," she said once we reached our table. "Can I start you off with some drinks?"

The restaurant was busy and she was obviously stressed, and I immediately felt bad for her. I remembered working at a restaurant at her age – 19, 20 – around there. It was the worst job of my life. But we need experiences like that, don't we? To grow?

"Water for me, please," I said, gesturing to Avery to go next.

"Coke."

He never said please or thank you. It was such a small thing but it grated on me. I smiled at the waitress, trying to silently apologize for his manners, or lack of them, and she smiled softly back.

Now for conversation.

Silence.

Silence.

Silence.

It felt like forever just staring at menus. I knew what I wanted immediately, and perhaps Avery did too, but admitting that meant giving ourselves the opportunity to talk and I, for one, had no interest in that. It wasn't that I didn't want to talk to Avery – it was that I had too much to say. You stop talking to someone you love for two reasons: Either you've run out of words or you have a surplus of them. There's no in between. The silence generated by each is threatening enough to a relationship, but the longer you wait, the worse it gets. All we did was wait. Wait for the other to start. Wait for the beginning of the conversation. Wait for the end.

"You have work tomorrow?" I decided to break the silence. It was a half-hearted attempt, but part of me felt a bit superior for putting in the effort, at least superficially.

"Yeah, 6-6."

"Damn. Long day."

"Yeah, but it'll be good money."

"Mhmm."

"Know what you're getting?"

"Yeah. The eggplant. What're you getting?"

"Fettucine."

I nodded. It felt like we were at a business meeting. Honestly, I probably would've felt more comfortable with a random colleague. Part of me wouldn't have been surprised if we'd thrown out phrases like "end of business today," "circle back," "thanks for handling," and "touch base." The sophisticated buzz words of people who know each other just well enough to communicate and not well enough to care.

"You look nice," he offered, tempering the uneasiness between us for a moment.

I was surprised. Compliments from Avery were few and far between. Usually I had to ask for them. *Do you like this dress? Does this necklace look good? Do you like these pants I bought?* Granted, my wardrobe was fairly limited. I wore uniforms three days a week and yogas most others, but occasionally I threw on a pair of sexy skinny jeans and a nice top just to see if he'd say something. He never did. Except tonight, I suppose. I'd settled on a sleek red dress and black leggings for the evening. The dress felt tight against my skin, restrictive, smothering.

"Thank you," I said. I yanked at the fabric at my stomach to give myself a little air, to no avail.

Neither of us said anything until the waitress came back. We ordered and settled into another uncomfortable silence, waiting for the food and a bit of inspiration to keep the night going.

I had no appetite. The eggplant came covered in thick bread-ing and smothered in marinara sauce, cheese melted in every crevice. It looked amazing. I just didn't have any desire to eat it. I did the little trick my mom taught me when I was a kid – *if you're eating at someone's house and you don't like what they give you, cut it into tiny pieces and move it around on your plate.* She used to tell me this like it was a novel idea she came up with all on her own. By the time Avery had finished his fettucine, my eggplant was in about 100 pieces. The waitress came back over and asked if we were done, and if we needed boxes, to which I politely declined.

"How was it?"

Eight years together and he still didn't know me well enough to pick up on little things.

"Fine. How was yours?" I barked back.

He just looked at me. Sometimes I heard myself and the way I talked to him. Every word was so angry. I didn't mean it to sound that way. But every so often it was like I'd see myself through his eyes and hear what I said to him from his perspective and I felt so ashamed. The worst part was, I had no idea how to *not* sound that way.

"I'm sorry."

I meant it. I *was* sorry. But I was also so *angry.*

I wanted to ask Avery if he remembered what the 9th was. If he'd thought about it like I had. If he'd gotten a sweet text to so kindly remind him of the day he was supposed to be a father. I was angry. Angry that he hadn't said something about it. Angry that I wanted him to. Angry that I didn't want him to.

Angry.

Angry.

Angry.

But all of that anger and the words that expressed it just sat on my tongue like dead weight. At the end of the day, they were just too heavy to heave up and out into the air between us. So I said "I'm sorry" and let the rest lay where it was. Where it had been for years.

He moved his hand across the table and held it out, palm up, inviting mine in. I put my hand in his and felt his soft, warm fingers curve over mine. I wish so much that I hadn't, but in that moment, all I could think of was how different Parker's hands felt. And how much I wanted those hands to be his.

S E S S I O N
T W O

———

"WHAT DOES IT MEAN FOR YOU to hear Avery say that?" Dr. Forner directed his gaze to me, fixing his eyes on mine in a way that, for some reason, made me feel the slightest bit unsettled.

I don't think we were ever really in love.

Those were Avery's exact words. What did the good doctor *think* it meant for me to hear him say that?

I was angry, partially because the sentiment stung, and partially because it was all too accurate. I looked around the room without moving my head. Somehow it felt like shifting my eyes might stop the tears from forming. Stupid tricks like that never work. I wiped two tears away from my eyes with my sleeve. I'd worn my good cardigan, the one that transitions well from spring to summer. It was a clear, cool day and the weather felt exactly how you'd expect the middle of March to be. The cardigan had been the perfect choice. It was yellow, the kind of color I'd never normally choose. But I'd worn it to my sister's first wedding – it paired perfectly with the navy bridesmaids dresses she'd picked out for her fall nuptials – and for some reason, I just liked it. I liked the way it fit – not too snug and not too loose. The yellow matched nicely with my blue jeans and blue flats. But now it had a smudge of mascara on the sleeve. *Figures.*

"Odette?"

In the midst of my half-hearted attempt at stopping myself from crying, I'd completely forgotten to answer Dr. Forner's question. He didn't seem irritated – just eager. Eager to get to whatever the core of our issue really was.

"I mean, it doesn't feel good."

"Can you be more specific? Do you agree with what he's saying? Do you think the two of you were ever in love? Even at the beginning?"

I paused and looked over at Avery. He was sitting closer to me this time, his left leg nearly touching my right. He had his head in his hands, his cheeks resting awkwardly on his palms. His eyes looked so, so sad.

"I think we were in love at the beginning maybe. I think we thought we were."

"What changed?"

What didn't?

"I mean, the baby."

Avery jumped up instantly, bounded over to the door and yanked it open.

"I'm done."

"Avery, please sit down." Dr. Forner's eyes were kind and forgiving, the kind that made it easy to feel heard, even when you yourself didn't want to listen.

"I'm *done*."

Avery wasn't just angry. He was hurt. Tears had already started gathering behind his eyes. His anger, I thought – I knew – was his way of forcing the pain away.

I didn't say anything. What was I supposed to say? We'd said everything to each other almost seven years ago. Now it was old news. It was long buried, but it was never gone. It hung around us everywhere we went. It painted the walls, over the bright white we'd picked out together. It fastened itself to the drapes and clung to the banisters. It stayed long after we wanted it gone. Some things never really leave, and grief is the most unwelcome of guests.

The funny thing was, which I'd only just realized as I watched Avery pace, distressed, from one end of the room to the other as Dr. Forner entreated him to stay, was that we'd never brought it up since. In all those days and all those fights, it had never once been mentioned. We hadn't talked about it, cried about it (together), argued about it. Nothing. Never. Not once.

"It looks like we've hit on something here. This is something we need to get through. This is obviously something that's causing you a great deal of stress," Dr. Forner said, motioning in Avery's direction.

"If I can just get you to sit down for a few minutes, we can take some breaths, recenter, refocus, and work through this trigger point."

Avery looked at me and I looked away. I couldn't stand to see him cry. I couldn't stand the idea that I'd caused him to. He breathed heavily, as if for the first time in minutes, and heaved himself back to the couch, this time sitting as far toward the other end of me as possible.

"Thank you, Avery," Dr. Forner said. "Let's try to continue."

I nodded and folded my hands in my lap. These were uncharted waters before us. For some reason, the moment made me remember a passage from a Shakespeare play (*was it Hamlet?*) I hadn't thought about in ages:

> *To grunt and sweat under a weary life,*
> *But that the dread of something after death,*
> *The undiscovered country from whose bourn*
> *No traveler returns, puzzles the will,*
> *And makes us rather bear those ills we have,*
> *Than fly to others that we know not of?*

The undiscovered country. No traveler returns. Shakespeare meant to describe death when he wrote that. He meant to say that the afterlife, whatever follows these waking hours, is no more than a world as yet unknown. How delightfully comforting it is to think of it that way, isn't it? That maybe the people we love aren't gone – they've just moved away.

"Odette," he continued, turning toward me. "I don't recall either of you mentioning you had children before. Can you tell me about this?"

In my high school English class sophomore year, we used to have to tell a story in five words or less. I suddenly wished I could tell this one under the same constraints.

"I guess."

I breathed in *hard*, so hard that my entire chest felt like it'd been impaled. It lasted a second, no longer, and then it was gone.

Here we go.

Dr. Forner looked at me, his eyes simultaneously reassuring me it was okay, and urging me to begin.

"Whenever you're ready."

———————

Over time, I've found that there are at least a hundred different ways to tell a story. Okay, that's hyperbole. There are several ways to tell any given story. Perspective makes a huge difference. Detail is similarly important. Most of the time, you tell it from your own side of the fence. It's not a bad thing – we describe things based on how we feel them. It's normal. But my perspective and Avery's were always so wildly different. It's not that they didn't align – it was like they never even shared the same space. They came from entirely different worlds.

Sitting in that awkwardly uncomfortable leather couch, I pretended to find words that had been on my tongue for seven years. I didn't need to look for them. In a way, they were waiting for me.

But even with those hundred plus ways to tell a story, sometimes you tell it in the worst possible way, simply because you don't have the energy to do it justice. And that is what happened on the brown leather couch, seated far from Avery, my hands sweating within their grasp, fingers intertwined so hard they felt like they might snap off. I found the words. I let the words go. And I said this instead:

"I was pregnant. It didn't work out."

Seven words. Almost made it. I would've lost the game.

Avery looked at me sharply, his eyes screaming through mine. I heard myself. I heard how flippant the words sounded as I said them. I didn't mean for them to sound that way. I meant to say so much more. So many things. So different. I meant for so many things to be different.

"Alright, what's happening between you two right now?" Dr. Forner asked, wheeling his chair out from behind his desk, closer toward us until it bumped up against the ottoman separating his side of the room from ours.

"Do you want to finish that?" Avery said, his eyes still fixed on mine, unblinking, completely focused.

I looked away.

"You can finish it."

I didn't mean to be difficult. But I also had no desire to go back to that place, the *undiscovered country*, as it were, in my mind that had been isolated for so long. I didn't want to travel back there. *Don't make me go back there.*

"Odette got pregnant a few months after we started seeing each other. That's the only reason we got married."

The only reason? I can remember other reasons. There were other reasons, weren't there?

"She wanted to have an abortion. She said she didn't want it. She was 21; I was 20. I was ready. I could've done it. I convinced her to keep it. Gracie, the baby – she was stillborn."

"Is there any blame there, Avery? Any blame you hold toward Odette that the baby didn't live?"

He didn't have to answer. He gave himself away immediately. Silence is such a snitch. It tells us more than words ever could.

What a massively irritating cliché.

I tried not to cry. I bit my lip and crammed my eyelids together. I pressed my nails into my palms until I could feel them start to bleed. But nothing worked. In the silence, as Avery looked at me and Dr. Forner looked at Avery and I looked at nothing, I cried. With no regard for my yellow cardigan and the black/brown supposedly waterproof mascara rolling down my cheeks and meshing with the fabric; with no care for how I looked or sounded; with no desire to stop or will to contain myself, I just cried. I didn't realize Avery was crying too until my breath caught up with me and I took a gasping inhale. I heard muted whimpers and, for a second, thought they were mine, until I saw Avery's shoulders shaking slightly back and forth. For what felt like hours, I sat there, Avery on one end of the couch sobbing silently, me on the other, Dr. Forner seated behind the ottoman, writing scribbles on his notepad.

Sometimes, those lost places in our minds don't need to be found again. Sometimes, they just need to be left alone.

CHAPTER
THREE

—————

"Do you wanna know what I think?" Parker leaned toward me, setting his elbows onto the desk and fitting his head into his cupped hands like a kid in middle school.

I felt myself smile. God I loved him.

"Sure."

"I think you like the attention."

"What attention?"

"You're always bitching about guys talking to you, hitting on you. I think you *like* it. Tell me I'm wrong."

"I don't like the attention. I like being able to do my job un-in-terr-up-ted." I emphasized each syllable, tapping his cheek with my finger with each beat.

He studied me, his eyes gently caressing each part of my face. It was right before shift change, before the previous shift was relieved and the new one, in this case ours, took over. This was our time – early mornings and late nights. Those were our moments. The office was conveniently tucked away, just enough so that we could get away with a little too much before anyone came around. But most of the time, we just talked. Being with him forced every painful moment between Avery and I out of my mind. I didn't have to think about it. I didn't have to live it. I was a different person there. At the station, to Parker, I was Lucy – strong, confident, *wanted*. With Avery, I was angry, introverted, vulnerable, guarded. There was such a difference – such a dramatic disparity between *Lucy* and *Odette*. I liked Lucy. I liked the woman I was with Parker. I liked leaving the baggage behind, even if it was just for 24 hours at a time.

"What?" I stroked the side of his face with my thumb. His cheeks were always so soft.

"Nothing," he whispered. He leaned in and kissed me.

Kissing him was like taking a first gulp of air after holding your breath. It was everything. There was never anything rushed about it. His lips slowly and cautiously wrapped around mine; his tongue wasn't forceful or prying. It was gradual, gentle, caressing. He kissed me like he loved me. He'd never said so. He always said the same thing when I said that word to him: "You know how I feel about you, Lucy."

I did. I thought I did. Sometimes I felt like I threw around "the L word" with reckless abandon and he withheld it with similar stringency. We were so opposite in that way. But he felt it. He had to feel it. The way he touched me, kissed me, held me – you don't do that if you don't love someone, right?

We heard shuffling on the stairs and pulled back quickly. I pushed my chair back and stood up as Rommie came charging in. He was possibly the least graceful person I'd ever met. He was shorter than the rest of the shift, maybe 5'7", and stocky, and he did everything with the refinement of a puppy seeing a mud puddle for the first time.

"LT, Carrigan. Just put a pot on if ya want any."

Rommie was always in a good mood. He never wavered. He was young, too young to be sullied by life or work or complication. He was 19 and as fresh and naïve as a person could be. Despite the fact that there was really no need to announce that fresh coffee had been brewed, he never once missed the opportunity to alert the entire shift, typically one by one, that he'd taken the initiative (as he was supposed to) and put one on. He didn't brag about anything else, which made it even more of a joke to the rest of the shift. The one thing he needed people to know he did was make the coffee in the morning.

I looked at Parker and he looked back at me and smiled just slightly.

"Thank you, Rommie," he said, "Make sure to tell everybody else so nobody misses a cup."

I knew he was joking. He knew he was joking. Rommie did not know he was joking. But regardless of whether he was in on the joke, he smiled broadly, said "aye aye, LT" and strode out.

As soon as he left, I sat back down. Parker chuckled and put his hand over his eyes.

"Jesus, he's as dumb as they come."

"Aw, he means well."

He looked at me and shook his head.

"That's why you're the nice one."

"Perhaps."

He took my hand and kissed it gently.

"Over/under 15 calls today. Go."

"Over. I say 7 on the engine, 10 on the ambo, 2 on the squad."

"No way. 4 engine, 7 ambulance, none on the squad."

"OK. We'll see who's right. What's the winner get?"

He stroked a nonexistent beard and made an exaggerated face to signify he was thinking incredibly deeply on the matter.

"If I win," he started, before switching to a whisper, "you wear the red one next shift." He motioned to his chest at the word "red."

The morning had officially started, which meant more discretion from both of us.

"Do what?" I said loudly in the most exaggerated voice I could muster. I liked toying with him, especially with things he couldn't say out loud.

He gave me a look of fake annoyance and typed on his phone before passing it off to me.

"THE RED BRA."

I laughed and put the phone back on the desk.

"I know, I know. OK, if I win, what do I get?"

"$15."

"Deal," I said, shaking his hand. "But you won't win. I'll probably just wear…"

His phone rang.

"Wife," the screen showed, lighting up with a picture of the two of them on their wedding day. I felt my whole body shudder.

"I've gotta," he started, motioning toward the phone.

"Yeah. Yeah. Of course."

I stood up and pushed the chair back into the desk. As I turned to walk out, I tried desperately to tune out the beginning of their conversation, but I couldn't.

"Hey love. How's your morning so far?"

I closed my eyes and moved as fast as I could down the hallway. He didn't sound like that with me. He didn't sound tired like that. Here, in this world, she was the other woman. She was the interloper, the intruder. Wasn't she?

That same day was the first time we ever ran a call together, oddly enough. Usually, I was on the ambulance and he was on the engine. Or I was on the engine and he was on the squad. It just never seemed to work out that we were both on the engine at the same time. That day, it did. And as if the fire gods chose our partnership to bless, we got a box at precisely 6:55 p.m. We had just finished up dinner and were clearing away the dishes, handing each one off to Rommie to wash and Andy, who everyone called Featherweight, to dry. (One thing I learned early on in my career, and that held true nearly five years after I started, was that if you can have a nickname, you will. Oftentimes, the nickname your shift assigns you will have absolutely nothing to do with your actual, given name. Usually it's related to something you did or said one time that somehow stuck. There were ten people on my shift, including me: Parker, the lieutenant, who was simply LT; Capt. Kenny Howe, who most of his peers called "'Stache," even though, to my knowledge, he'd never had a moustache; Technician Damian Dawson, who we called "Daws;" Technician Delano "Deli" Diaz; Firefighter Teddy "Stern" Sterner; Kendrick "Vick" Vickers; Carter Tamwell, who everyone called "Felix" because once in the academy an officer had mistaken him for another recruit and called him Felix, and of course, it stuck; Franklin "Rommie" Romanowski; and Andy "Featherweight" Taylor. "Featherweight" was so chosen because he was a remarkably tall and lanky individual with a startlingly low body fat percentage).

That night, I had Parker and Daws on the engine with me.

You couldn't pick a better crew. The three tones sounded right as I was passing a fork off to Rommie. I dropped it and ran, nearly tumbling over Daws on the way to the stairs. Running behind Parker on the way to the engine took maybe 15 seconds, but it was long enough to give me unfamiliar and unsettling anxiety. I'd never seen him in action, so to speak. He was an officer, but hardly ever really *my* officer. He was and he wasn't. I took his orders better in bed than I did on the fireground, simply because I'd never had to on an actual incident. The idea of him being my CO was unfamiliar and a little daunting. That's probably why relationships like ours are so frowned upon. Don't shit where you eat, so they say.

I'd already gotten my turnout pants and hood on before we sped through the bay doors, but I fumbled with my radio strap trying to get it on. Something about having him with me was tripping me up. Like I was looking to impress him or something. He looked back at me while putting his gear on and tapped his helmet, signifying that his helmet cam was on. He was thoroughly obsessed with taking video footage of every fire call, and from what dispatch was relaying on the radio, it was looking like an actual, honest-to-god blaze. Real fires are a lot more rare than people think. Most of the time, we run medical calls and fire alarms and any related assortment of bullshit. Real fires are few and far between and always 100 percent worth the effort spent putting them out.

We arrived first on scene running first-due. It was a detached rancher, fire showing from the alpha side. Parker – Lt. Kane – didn't have to tell me to pull a line. I already knew. I hopped out and mounted the side of the engine, leaning over to steady myself.

I pulled the crosslay and ran it down to the front door while he did a 360. Fire and dark black smoke were rippling angrily out of the windows on one side as if frantically escaping a space they'd quickly outgrown. I called for water and started advancing the line, noticing quickly that Parker had picked it up behind me and was heaving it in the doorway after me. I had never been afraid of fire before. And this one, though mildly impressive, was hardly a showstopper. But for some reason, I felt scared. As soon as I entered the house and lost visibility, I became acutely aware of the sweat quickly saturating the inside of my uniform, and the stale smell of air from my cylinder. I stopped. I got a few steps in and stopped. I didn't mean to; it just happened. Over the sound of my own breathing and radio traffic, I heard muffled yells just before I felt a tug on my pack.

"What's going on? Keep moving!"

I felt frozen. In that moment, for some reason I still can't quite understand, all I could imagine was Avery sitting in Dr. Forner's office, crying loudly into his hands, saying over and over again, "I just feel so relieved that she's gone."

A strong push from Parker startled my mind out of its anxiety-riddled sojourn, and I was suddenly back on task.

Everything after that felt like a blur. Parker didn't say anything to me until we got back to the station. He asked to see me in the office and closed the door.

"What the fuck happened today?"

I'd seen him angry before, but never with me. It was always someone pissing him off or irritating him, but never me. Today, it was me.

"I don't know. I froze. I don't know what happened."

Some part of me expected concern from the man I'd grown so close to. But this Parker and my Parker were different people, and there was no sympathy to be had. There was a lieutenant chastising a firefighter, and that's all.

He started to say something and held his hand up, waving it back and forth as if to signal frustration so significant he couldn't put it into words.

"Just go."

I didn't argue with him. I didn't quite understand his reaction. Yes, I fucked up. No, I shouldn't have. But disappointment and concern seemed like more reasonable responses than anger. At least, for *my* Parker.

The next morning, we both wandered to our cars at the same time. I wanted to tell him I was right about the number of calls. I won the bet. But he was looking down, texting and walking at the same time, half-aware of the foot traffic around him as shift change brought new blood and a fresh crew. No doubt talking to his wife, exchanging "good mornings" and "I miss yous." I missed that from Avery. I missed that in general. For a moment, I was jealous of Parkers' wife, not for having Parker, but for having *someone*.

CHAPTER
FOUR

———

I STARED AT MY PHONE: 09:47. Usually, I tried to sleep after coming home from shift. You never get restful sleep at a fire station, even if no calls come in overnight. It's like your body is always half-awake, half-listening, half-preparing. Your mind is always ready even if your body isn't. You might sleep, but there's a part of you constantly poised for action, conscious of the voices calling out over dispatch and whatever disasters or idiotic exploits of human stupidity they set out for you.

But lately, I couldn't sleep when I got home either. I could only look at my phone and wait for messages that I knew wouldn't come. We didn't text each other or talk much outside of work. It just wasn't something we did. We had never decided that, Parker and I. We had never sat down and had a conversation about when we would communicate with each other. We just knew. What we had was almost exclusively at work and, aside from rare messages, communication was limited to the station or in person. But god, I missed him. I missed his hands, always calloused and yet somehow always soft. I missed the way he threw his head back when he laughed and the way he looked at me from across a room and winked. I missed the way he could claim me as his without even saying a word.

We hadn't gotten any calls after the box, thankfully, but I wasn't been able to get back to sleep. Parker and I didn't say anything to each other after we spoke in the office, and he'd left the station by the time I got out of bed. For some reason, despite our unspoken rule, I was hoping he'd text. Waiting two more days to get any sort of resolution, or know he wasn't mad at me, seemed impossible.

I hated that so much of myself was wrapped up in what he thought. Why wasn't I like that with Avery? I used to care more what Avery thought. When did I stop? Our next therapy session wasn't for another four days, and part of me dreaded it, but part of me was anxiously waiting for it to come around. We hadn't said a word to each other since the last session, not even "good morning" or "thanks for the coffee." He went to work earlier than he needed to and came home after I was already in bed. We didn't text while I was at the station at all. Our lives, outside of therapy, were entirely separate. I wondered how much of his time was spent with whomever was comforting him, and I questioned if he thought the same about me. I never worried about being "caught." I honestly can't say that I cared. Maybe part of me wanted him to find out, whether to tell me to stop or to cut me loose.

◆ ◆ ◆

Avery and I had two dogs. One was a golden retriever, Leo, and the other was a Yorkshire terrier, Camden. Camden was infinitely louder than Leo. Whenever I got home from the station, I would lay down on the couch and stare at the ceiling, or my phone, or the tv, usually with nothing on it. Leo would sleep on the floor beside me, but only so long as I had one hand on his back. And Camden would post up on my chest and snore away as I pet his tiny head.

In that exact position, I stroked Leo's back with one hand and stared at my phone, propped up against Camden's stomach, while petting him with the other. I was lost in reruns of the final moments of the last therapy session. It's funny how sometimes our minds are more entertaining, whether positively or negatively, than any form of media. We can torture ourselves with remembrances so brilliantly. There was no Parker at home, no station to distract me from the realities happening around me. The phone rang and Camden barked loudly, sending it spinning like a top straight to the floor. I gasped and put my hand to my chest, closing my eyes to regroup and contain the sudden jolt of panic that only a spontaneous, unexpected call can deliver. More surprising than the ringtone, perhaps, was the caller. Parker.

I thought maybe it was a misdial. Or, worse, his wife. I almost didn't answer it. But it was Parker's phone regardless, so I did.

"Hello?"

I sounded even more tentative than I'd intended.

"Lucy. Let's meet up today."

That was a first. Any time we saw each other outside of the station was right before or right after a shift, or at a time we determined while together. We never called each other to set something up. That would be altogether too dangerous. Call logs are serious things, and nothing to be taken lightly. But apparently, that day, Parker was taking things a bit more lightly than usual.

"OK. When? Today?"

"Yeah. Can I come to your place?"

There was something weird about him coming over. It was still Avery's house as much as mine. The idea of having another man in our home, let alone our bed, was unsettling, regardless of our situation or how we felt about each other. Like there are rules of combat, there are rules of infidelity. There are things you do and things you don't do.

"Not a good idea."

"Please."

I closed my eyes tight. Avery wouldn't be home for another several hours, later if he stayed out like he usually did after work. I could obey the rules, the bare minimum of respect toward any partner, and lose time with Parker, or I could say fuck it and tell him to come over. I lost either way.

He's probably fucking somebody else anyway. Do you seriously think he hasn't brought her over here when you're on shift? Come on. Be real.

"OK. Can you be here in half an hour?"

"Yeah, I'll be right over."

I said OK and hung up. I realized immediately I was completely unprepared for company, even if it was just Parker. I had an inherent need to be my best at all times for him, and the house being a complete shambles was hardly my best.

I quickly brushed my hair and my teeth and put on a tiny bit of mascara and eye liner. That would have to do. I had to change, so I opted for leggings and an oversized flannel, with my red bra and black lace thong underneath. I imagined something would happen and I wanted to be prepared. He certainly wasn't coming over just to talk. I tidied up the house as much as I could. I moved Avery's shoes from in front of the door to inside the coat closet.

And, in a move that surprised even myself, turned our wedding picture on the dresser over. What I was doing was wrong. In any situation, it was wrong. But it didn't feel like it. I didn't feel angry with myself for being with Parker. I didn't feel much of anything. I did, but I didn't. Anything negative I started to feel I shoved down inside myself like I was trying to stuff an oversized trash bag. The more that crept out, the more I crammed back down. I felt the desire to be desired, the need to be held and wanted. I felt a longing for connection, to be touched and felt and seen. I needed Parker. I was on autopilot, going with the flow and following someone else's navigation.

The door rang and I sprinted over to open it. There was Parker, standing with a box of truffles. He was wearing dark jeans, a dark blue shirt that made his eyes pop even more, and a brown leather jacket.

"Special delivery."

"You or the chocolates?"

He smiled and tossed the chocolates onto the floor before quickly picking me up and kissing me.

"Where's the bedroom?"

"Upstairs. Last door at the end of the hallway."

"Well let's go then."

He hoisted me up so my legs wrapped around his waist and kissed my neck while he carried me up the stairs. By the time we reached the bedroom, my shirt was off. He set me down gently on the bed and positioned himself on top of me, stroking my arms one at a time as he kissed me. He was so, so gentle. We'd had sex before, but it was at the station or in one of our cars – the quick and dirty version. Passionate, but cautious. The "in and out" version of making love required when doing so is a fire-able offense, or getting caught is a realistic possibility. This time was different. He was slow, methodical. He took my pants off as if in slow motion, feeling every part of me with his hands, his mouth. I closed my eyes. Everything about it was right. I felt him slide inside me and my whole body shivered; every part of me felt him. He pulled me close and held me and, in those beautiful moments, I felt like I was completely his.

There are different kinds of sex. There's fucking and there's making love. This was the ladder. His body said he loved me even though his words never had.

When we were done, he kept holding me for what felt like hours. I didn't feel discarded or used; I felt a clear, defined sense of connectedness. There was no "him" and "me"; there was just "us."

We lay there naked with the sheets pulled over us, not saying anything. Finally, I broke the silence.

"Why did you come over here?"

"For that."

"But you never do this. *We* never do this."

"We do now."

"Are you OK?"

He seemed much more devil-may-care than usual. He stared off into space and stroked my arm as I lay on his chest, looking up at him.

"You're a woman. Explain this to me."

I propped up on my elbow and waited.

"So I specifically told my wife I didn't want to have dinner with her family, right? And she goes ahead and makes plans for us *on the day we work.* And then gets mad at me for not taking off. I mean she said she mentioned it a few months ago and I should've remembered. But I told her I didn't want to go!"

I pulled the sheets higher over my chest and scooted away from him. I never brought up Avery to him. I kept everything separate. I hated when he brought up his wife. I didn't understand how he did it. How could he have sex with me like that and then talk about a completely irrelevant argument *that he had with his wife?* He'd done that before – randomly ranted about her to me after kissing me or touching me. And I'd asked him before how he did it – thinking about both of us at the same time when I so clearly separated everything. Or I had, until that day, I suppose.

"Compartmentalization," he'd say. "I can keep things separate in my head. I don't know. It's just how I operate."

I wanted to kick him out of bed. I wanted to yell at him, to tell him how incredibly insensitive it was to bring her up when he was with me. But I couldn't do that. And a part of me kind of felt like I did the same. There was me with Parker and me with Avery, and though I wasn't quite so brazen about it, in a way, I did the same thing Parker did. I broke things up in my mind to make them more palatable for myself. To explain things away to the jury in my head, defending myself to an imaginary audience that required no such justification.

"I mean, if she told you a while ago you probably should've taken off."

"You think? I don't know. I don't get women."

He pulled me back towards him and kissed my forehead.

Compartmentalization, huh?

We lay there for a few more minutes until he looked at his phone.

"I should get going."

We both got dressed and he picked up his wallet and keys from the nightstand. Avery's nightstand.

"Walk me out?"

"Of course."

Everything about this was weird. And despite how hurt I was, I wanted him to stay more than anything in the world.

He kissed me on the cheek and grabbed my ass before walking out.

"See you in two days, doll."

I smiled and closed the door behind him. I went upstairs to re-make the bed and purge any evidence of his presence. It wasn't until after he left that I realized neither of us had brought up the call yesterday, or his reaction in the office, or the lack of communication between then and his phone call. There was something so perfectly unexpected about Parker that it almost – almost – made sense. Nothing about him was predictable. He was, in every way, a walking contradiction – a paradox of a human if ever there was one. He had hard and fast rules until he didn't. His resolve was unwavering until it wasn't. He'd been that way since we started this, whatever this was, in February. Looking back, it had been so innocent at first. He was just so easy to talk to, so open and genuine and kind. Office chats were our thing long before we slept together. And then, one day, he put his hand on mine and said "Lucy," and looked directly into my eyes and kissed me. And I felt like that kiss was the most predestined event of my entire life. And then we were just us. And then, he was leaving my house and I was perfectly fine. Perfectly fine until I turned the picture of me and Avery back upright and suddenly, staring at our smiling faces, me in my wedding gown, incredibly pregnant, and him in a suit and tie, I felt myself fall to the floor. I sobbed there for hours, not the quiet, ladylike sobs you do in public, but the raw, real, primal cries that come from somewhere incredibly deep inside you. Everything I'd done with Parker was once so natural with Avery. Right here in this room, on this bed. I'd stared at that same ceiling and clung to his bare back as he moved inside me. We'd been in love in that room. We'd been us in that room. It wasn't being with Parker that made my stomach churn. It was being with Parker *in that room, in our house* – the house where we'd expected Gracie. The house we'd come home to without her, without a little girl to love and hold and soothe and annoy as she moved from baby to toddler to tween to teen to adult. Parker was my home away from home, but he wasn't my home here. He was a foreign presence, a reminder of the brokenness not just around me, but inside me. The brokenness that would never be healed.

I ran to the bathroom and flung the toilet open, throwing up violently, as if my body was trying to cleanse itself of the last few hours. But it couldn't work like that. And I cried. I cried as I got undressed and stepped in the shower. I cried while I washed him off of me, feeling a mixture of regret and sadness – a part of me longing to keep Parker's scent on me for just a little bit longer; a part of me praying to expel it. So much contradiction can exist in one's mind at one time. So much confusion.

I went to bed early that night. I heard Avery come in and set his things down on the counter. I heard him creep up the stairs slowly and shower in the guest bedroom. And, I was surprised when I felt him kiss my cheek before going back down the stairs to sleep on the couch. It was so unexpected that part of me wondered if I'd dreamed it – some half-awake imagining of a better time come to haunt me, or comfort me..

I cried softly into my pillow until I fell asleep. That night, I dreamed I was floating between two houses. One was old and falling apart, its walls eaten alive by termites and water and erosion of years, with no sign of maintenance or care at all. And the other was brand new, shiny appliances and fresh paint throughout. I floated and floated, trying desperately to land in one or the other. But no matter how hard I tried, I couldn't set myself down in either one – I just kept floating between them.

SESSION
THREE

"OUR LAST SESSION WAS VERY EMOTIONAL for the two of you. How have you communicated since then?"

Not at all. Null. Nada. Nothing. Radio silence.

"We've both been working a lot," Avery said – an excuse I would've used if I'd answered first. At least we still had that – similar minds; similar lies.

Dr. Forner nodded.

"I know this is painful for both of you, but it's important that we explore the issues at the core of the *challenges* that you're facing as a couple."

He emphasized the word "challenges," as if he wanted us to take note of it specifically. He always said "challenges" instead of "problems," as if that made it any better. He'd called me out on that once.

"Odette, let's try using the term *challenges* instead, alright? Language is so important to our subconscious, and we don't want to reinforce that either of you are the quote-unquote problem."

I'd wanted to say that both of us *were* the problem, but I didn't. I'd just nodded and said OK and since then, problems were challenges and arguments were opportunities.

"Take me back to the beginning. Do you remember how you felt when you first saw each other? Avery, do you want to go first?"

Avery looked at me for a quick second and then looked away, as if the sight of me was too painful for him. Maybe it was. I examined the walls, waiting for him to start. Every time I sat in that office I seemed to notice something new. This time, it was a large painting of a woman staring at her reflection in a puddle. She had wavy brown hair that fell to her shoulders, with a little red fascinator on her head that matched her dress, which fell just below her ankles. She was barefoot, and her feet had collected the tiniest bit of mud on each side. Her face wasn't visible -- even in the puddle it was hidden, like the artist wanted you to see your own in its place -- yet I somehow felt sad for her, as if I could feel her heartbreak through the canvas. Which struck me as odd, simply because I had no way of knowing if the painter meant for her to be a sympathetic subject or not. I just, for some reason, felt a sense of desolation looking at it. I wondered how I hadn't noticed it the first two times I was there.

"When we met, I was working at a convenience store and she was working at Starbucks, I think. Or a restaurant. Something like that. She worked two jobs around then. Whichever it was – I remember it was next to my job, so she'd always make an excuse to come see me. I can't remember which place it was at the time..."

"I didn't need an excuse," I said, interrupting him. "I really needed things!"

He looked at me, mildly playfully, as if forgetting we were on opposite sides of the war, and continued.

"Anyway, she would come over all the time and eventually it just became our thing. We would take our breaks together every day. I think when I first saw her, I remember her hair was pink." He laughed. "It was very, very pink."

I had completely forgotten about that. I hadn't thought about us at that age in so long. I smiled, anxiously waiting for him to continue as if he was telling a story I'd never heard before. As if he wasn't describing us, but some adorable, nauseatingly sweet couple in a romantic love story brought to life in a way only The Big Screen could do.

"I thought she was beautiful. I told her dumb jokes all the time just so she'd laugh. I loved her laugh."

I caught his perhaps subconscious use of the past tense, and it hit me harder than I was prepared for.

"Avery, was there a moment you fell in love with Odette?" Dr. Forner asked. "Maybe a time you remember feeling like you were connecting with her on that deeper level for the first time?"

Avery sat back. He'd been leaning forward as he spoke, resting his elbows on his knees. He seemed to relax more as he thought.

"She brought me a coffee," Avery started. "Decaf with two cream. And a chocolate chip cookie. And I hadn't asked for either. She just brought it one day on our break. It was so sweet. I'd only told her how I took my coffee, maybe once? I don't know. But she was just so sweet. I remember thinking – I know it's pretty fucking stupid – but I remember thinking I wanted to marry her right then and there. Maybe three weeks after we'd started talking. I just thought, 'I want this girl for the rest of my life.'"

I stared at the painting on the wall, watching the colors blend together as my eyes slowly filled with tears. He hadn't ever told me any of that. Last session he said we'd gotten married out of necessity, not desire. I never knew he wanted me like that.

"Odette," Dr. Forner turned to me. "How does hearing all of that make you feel?"

I cleared my throat. The painting looked like a jumbled mess of color now – the woman had all but disappeared into the puddle she once surveyed so intently.

"I never knew any of that," I said. "I mean, I knew what happened, obviously. But I didn't know he wanted to marry me then, or that he knew he loved me when I brought him coffee."

"Do you remember when you first felt that for Avery?" Dr. Forner asked.

I tried to think of those days – Odette and Avery: The Early Years. But it was like my brain couldn't latch onto any specific memories. I could remember feelings – how it felt to be young and excited about love, like it was a waterfall in constant motion, perpetually refilling for the both of us. But I couldn't connect with a single instance or situation or experience. It was like listening to a conversation through a wall, pressing my ear up to it just to hear muffled voices and far away sounds.

Say something. Say something. Say something.

I felt myself start to sweat as I sat there. I knew I had to get something out – Avery said all that. How could I have nothing to say? How could I not have a single memory – even a fallback memory that wasn't *the real moment*. It didn't have to be the epic, fall in love moment. Just *something*.

But there was nothing. My mind was blank.

"Odette?" Dr. Forner said, looking at me with eyes that seemed to plead with me to push some response out of the depths of my brain.

"I…I need more time."

Avery shook his head and buried it in his hands.

"She needs more time," he said, more to himself, it seemed, than anyone in the room. "More time for what? What does that say about us? About *you?* About how you feel *about me?*"

He was looking at me now, his eyes a mixture of pain and anger. Books always liken angry blue eyes to ominous clouds or storm-addled ocean waves, but his reminded me more of the deep dark of fresh blueberries, as weird as that might sound. There was something lively in them always. Even when they were hurt, they exuded *life.*

"I'm sorry. You know I can't always think on the spot like this."

"This isn't a pop quiz, Odette," Avery said. "It's one single time in our lives. One memory."

"I know. I'm sorry."

Dr. Forner, as if finally reading the room, picked that moment to leave off. He told me to use that as homework, to try to think of my "a-ha" moment for Avery.

"Avery, try not to hold this against Odette," he said. "It might be easy for you to remember these details, but trauma can cause a lot of suppression of even pleasant memories. Let's remember to be kind to one another, and meet each other where the other is, not where you want them to be. Good job today, both of you. I'll see you next week."

We walked out together, but in all the ways that matter, separately. We'd taken two cars – he had to get to work and I had to get back home – and neither of us said anything when we parted ways in opposite directions, him toward his Chevy Silverado, and me toward my Jeep.

The funny thing is, I thought of my memory almost as soon as we walked outside. It was about a week after we'd started talking. We were listening to music in his car, eating cheeseburgers and fries, and trying to finish a crossword puzzle before we both had to clock back in to our respective jobs. He was looking down at the puzzle, utterly confused but in no way defeated by it. He scratched his forehead with what he thought was the cap of the pen, only it was the wrong side and his mistake had led to several tiny ink lines on his skin. I laughed immediately, spitting half my bite of burger out of my mouth at the same time.

"What, you dork?" He laughed, pointing at the splattered food on the floor of the car.

"Your face!" I said in between giggles.

He looked in the mirror and started laughing.

"You think THAT'S funny?"

He picked up the pen and started drawing all over his face, little circles and smiley faces on his forehead and cheeks, and a fake mustache over his lip.

I gasped.

"You have to go back to work, Avery!"

"Eh, fuck it. What're they gonna do?"

I laughed so hard my stomach hurt and I couldn't finish the rest of my lunch, but I didn't care. I was just so incredibly happy. And, in that moment, looking at him with his ink-covered face, I thought to myself, "I fucking love this man."

And I really did. I really, really did.

CHAPTER
FIVE

———

THE END OF MARCH MEANT TWO THINGS: The annual March Madness prank contest at the station, and my wedding anniversary. We hadn't done anything for our anniversary in years. Usually, I'd get Avery a card and he'd give me a kiss on the cheek. Some years we had sex, but that hadn't been the case for the last few anniversaries. In an effort to avoid the date entirely, I chose to focus exclusively on the prank contest. It had been started by Daws when he became a firefighter and he'd taken it with him to every station he'd worked at since. The rules were simple: There were no rules. The last shift day of March, gloves came off, human decency was thrown out the window (as if it really existed in the fire department), and everything (and I mean everything) was fair game.

Pranks in the past had ranged from the milder ones done by sheepish rookies, like hiding someone's water jug or replacing flour with powdered sugar in pancakes, to the more calculated, reckless ones by senior firefighters, like soaking someone's clothes in the toilet and then putting the very saturated garments under their bed sheets, or filling turnout boots with ice. Some of them were so extreme, we actually got the battalion chief to write a disciplinary letter to the entire shift, which many took as a badge of honor (a rumor circulated at some point that the letter had been framed and hung up somewhere. That was never confirmed, though). Since then, there was a strict code of silence associated with the contest. Nothing that happened within the walls of the station as part of the prank war could be shared or disseminated with anyone outside of the shift. If someone was stationed there on overtime or detail, someone not usually on our shift, we had them sign a non-disclosure agreement. It was, in every sense, as legit as it could get.

We usually picked our victims and, most of the time, the same three or four people got pranked every time. Occasional shift changes meant new blood, but the core group remained the same. As the sole woman on the shift, I was the victim every year. Officers were strictly off limits. This was an unspoken, but incredibly clear rule that we all adhered to with the utmost stringency. Besides me, one of the younger guys was always a victim of the prank war. This time around, it was Rommie. Stern was a classic pretty boy in every sense of the phrase and so, because of his incredible propensity for believing anything anyone said, he was also always on the receiving end of the war.

Usually, the end of month prank extravaganza was a nice distraction from the mundanity, and occasional extreme stress, of the job. This time around, it was more than that. It was an escape. I didn't care if I was the victim in every single prank. I just wanted a little reprieve from everything going on around me and in my head. When we talk about things cutting like knives, we always think about negatives: words, actions, choices. But what about laughter? Laughter has the power to cut through awkwardness, irritability, shame, anger, distress, despair. Anything. Laughter can, in any real way, save lives. I needed that. The prank war was like a knife cutting through the thick fog of normal life.

I was sitting at the kitchen table drinking coffee when Rommie came bounding in, happy as ever. He was new to the prank war. He didn't know what to expect. In a way it was cute, the fact that he was so blissfully clueless. And, in other ways, I felt incredibly sorry for him for the 23 hours he had ahead – the torment he knew nothing about. He grabbed a mug off the table, already filled with coffee, and started pouring creamer he'd fetched from the fridge into it.

"You're not gonna check that?" I asked.

"Check what?"

"The coffee."

"Check it for what?"

"You know what today is, right?"

"Yeah. Prank day."

I leaned in and started to whisper.

"Rommie. I don't mean to scare you, but, just looking out for you, check the coffee. Nothing is safe. Trust me."

He laughed. "I'm sure I'll be fine. It can't be *that* bad."

I leaned back and took a sip from my own mug before putting both feet up on the chair across from me.

"Alright. Good luck. Don't say I didn't warn ya."

I alerted every rookie the morning of the Prank Wars. None of them ever listened. In truth, my cautionary spiel was somewhat part of it. Seeing them get more and more squirmy as the day went on was never *not* funny. I knew what to expect. I knew to check my coffee, my snacks before I ate them, my gear before I put it on, my bunk before I got in it, the toilet before I went to the bathroom, the hallways before I walked down – everything. In truth, they still got me. But I was cautious nonetheless, and I'd actually caught a few over the years.

I was halfway through a sip of coffee, and Rommie was just finishing his second creamer pour when we heard Stern's unmistakable voice yell, "Are you fucking kidding me?!"

"And so it begins," I said, gulping down the last of my coffee, scalding though it was, before running down to the bunk room. Half the shift was already assembled around Stern's bed when I got there. At first, all I saw were backs, and then, after strategically positioning myself between Daws and Parker, I saw it. There was Stern, his hands and hair both a bright, stunningly stark blue. Apparently someone, who was not yet willing to come forward, replaced the hair gel he used every morning with paint. There he stood, frantically and fruitlessly trying to rub it out with a bath towel.

Really, it was his own fault. We all constantly razzed him for wearing hair gel in the first place, let alone so much of it. But he chose to anyway, and this was the result.

"This better fucking rinse out."

The juxtaposition of his blue hair and very, very red face was almost comical.

"I look like a fucking idiot. Who was it?"

He scanned the amused faces one by one, but no one would fess up. The laughter, which seemed to intensify in waves, only made him more upset.

Rommie came up behind me.

"He looks like a smurf!" He half-yelled, half-snorted.

I burst out laughing.

"Rommie, shut the hell up."

Stern tossed the towel onto his bed and huffed his way to the bathroom.

"This better fucking rinse out. This better fucking rinse out. This better fucking rinse out." He chanted to himself as if willing the blue paint to somehow remove itself by osmosis.

As soon as he left, the captain turned to all of us, his arms folded like a disapproving father.

"OK, who did it?"

Parker chuckled and walked away immediately, leaving five of us standing with Captain Howe. I looked at Rommie, who looked at Daws who looked at Taylor who looked at Vick who looked back at me.

The captain didn't particularly care for jokes, pranks, or anything that involved any amount of joviality. But he didn't readily disapprove of any of it either. He usually just did something like that – a mild display of irritation, followed by exactly what he did next – a heavy sigh, turn and walk in the opposite direction, removing himself from any and all shenanigans.

"Worth it," Vick said under his breath. The rest of us laughed and hustled off in different directions as Stern continued cussing at the paint in the bathroom.

Surprisingly, the rest of the day's pranks were uncharacteristically tame. It was like creativity took a vacation for the year's games. Daws replaced the salt with sugar and vice versa, and he also put Crisco on the toilet seat right before Stern's mid-afternoon 10-minute bathroom session, which was only ever interrupted by a call and nothing else.

Stern had a rough day.

Vick put ketchup in Diaz's shaving cream bottle; Felix hacked into Deli's phone and changed all of his contacts to "That Bitch," and he also put all of my bedding inside different ceiling tiles throughout the station, so I had to hunt for them for at least 20 minutes before bed.

My sole prank of the day was pouring water, followed quickly by flour, all over Daws. He laughed more than I did.

Some days are just better than others. Prank Day was always one of those days.

◆ ◆ ◆

When the dust – and the flour – had settled, Parker and I sat in the office for our evening chat. It was a tradition, something we did every shift like clockwork. Of course, depending on calls, it ranged from 5 p.m. to midnight, and sometimes even later, but we always made time for it. It was our only dedicated time together.

Neither of us had brought up his visit since it happened, and for a weird couple of days, part of me wondered if I'd imagined the whole thing, or perhaps dreamed it. But I hadn't made it up. It had happened, for whatever reason. Maybe he was particularly mad at his wife, maybe he had a moment of weakness, or maybe his "give a fuck" just gave out for a few hours. Since then, I had tried desperately to forget about it, and yet held onto every sensation it gave me simultaneously. I regretted it, and yet I didn't. I wanted more, and I hated that I wanted more. What we had at the station was rushed, hurried. Even when we met outside the station, we were vigilant and somewhat hasty. Although the limited time was frustrating, it was also special – something uniquely ours – and sexy. Sexy because it was wrong. Wrong because we were working. Wrong because it was prohibited to sleep with your boss, let alone do it at work. But I tried not to think about any other reason it might be wrong, any other connections either one of us may have – *did* – have that made it wrong, rather than just by way of regulations. I tried not to think about it and, most of the time, I succeeded. It's funny how the mind works. So much can be shut out – so many emotions thrown aside. When I was younger, even in my early 20s, the idea of *having an affair* was so off my radar, so entirely *other* to me, that I would've laughed if someone had told me I became that. I did that. I was that person. I would've scoffed and walked away. *Not me*. But there I was, sitting across from Parker, holding his hand and caressing each finger one by one with my thumb, looking into his beautiful, soul-enlivening eyes, talking about trips we wanted to take together to New York and California and Ireland – trips we would never be able to take.

"I'm going to Rhode Island this weekend."

I stopped touching him and let his hand slip out of mine.

"How long will you be gone?"

"Just a week. The wife wants to go."

"Oh."

"So I'll be gone a few shifts."

"Okay. When we you going to tell me?" The question even surprised me as I said it. He wasn't mine. He had no obligation to tell me his personal schedule, where he went and when – or with whom. But I was hurt. Hurt because he hadn't told me. Hurt because he wasn't going with me, never mind the fact that he couldn't.

"Now."

I sat back and looked around the room. The station wasn't the same without him. I wasn't the same without him.

"Aw…are you gonna miss me?"

He smiled and cupped his hand around my cheek.

"You know the answer to that, Parker."

"That's Lieutenant Kane to you," he smirked.

"Yeah, right, so sorry, Loooo-tenant Kane."

He leaned in and kissed me slowly. His tongue moved in gentle circles in my mouth, painting a portrait I could only feel with my own.

"Yes, I'll miss you," I said.

"You'll be fine, Lucy."

I smiled at him, a fake, flat smile that even the most obtuse of men could see right through. I was upset that he was going to be gone, but more than that, I was disappointed that I wouldn't get to talk to him for seven days. Because we didn't text hardly at all when we weren't at the station. And I knew he wouldn't take the risk of getting caught by his wife. Parker was the distraction I needed to survive. Without him, I was like a deer left in an open field before a dozen hunters. I didn't stand a chance.

"What do you think happens when you die?" I asked him.

"Well that's random."

"I know. I've just been thinking about it."

"You OK?"

"Yeah. It's just this time of year."

Parker was the only one I'd told about Gracie. No one else in the station knew. I trusted him to keep it, like us, a secret.

He sighed and tapped his knee to signal me to sit on his lap. I moved over to him quickly and took my place where I felt I belonged, most sincerely, in every way. I let myself fall into his chest and he rested his chin on my forehead, stroking my hair with his free hand.

"I think, when we die, we exist in the minds of the people who loved us. I don't think that ever goes away."

I felt little tears drop slowly down my cheeks and come to rest on his PT shorts, making dark marks on the gray fabric. I remembered one day, right after we'd lost Gracie, when I'd wanted so badly to be held. To be welcomed into a space only two broken souls healing from the same grief can occupy. But there was no space for me and Avery. There was space for him, and there was space for me. It was like we'd rather drown in two adjacent boats, staring at one another, then go down together.

Like Rose and Jack. There was enough room on that damn door.

Only we weren't in a movie where romance means losing someone and gaining a sense of self. We were existing in Real Life, where your sense of self can be crushed a million times over and not a soul will notice, not even the ones closest to you. Rose and Jack struggled to survive, and Jack sacrificed himself to save the woman he loved. Avery didn't sacrifice for me. He didn't give up his raft for me. He pushed me onto mine, grabbed his own, and paddled to safety. He never looked back for me. He hadn't looked back for me since.

We sat in silence, Parker and I, his hand moving from my hair to my cheeks, wiping the tears away gently and slowly, without once asking me to stop crying.

Space.

With Parker, we had space. And we existed in it together.

We stayed that way for another half hour, until he gently nudged me and said it was time for bed. He kissed me on my forehead and took my head in his hands, looking intently into my eyes.

"You're stronger than you think, Lucy."

In that moment, a week without him felt like an eternity.

In the morning, he handed me a note discretely before he left. I waited until I got to my car to open it.

"Don't miss me too much, Lucy. Be back in a flash. You're perfect. Don't forget that."

I folded the note and put it in my pocket.

Seven days to go.

SESSION

FOUR

———

Two days to go. Two days to go. Two days to go.

I picked at a loose thread on my black knit sweater and repeated the countdown over and over in my head as I waited for Avery to arrive. He was late – not uncommon for him. Avery was historically late to everything. He'd been late to our wedding even, arriving after all of the groomsmen and half the guests. He hadn't even gotten dressed yet. I can't remember what his excuse was at the time, but it didn't matter. Nor did it matter as I sat on the couch in the therapist's office, yanked too hard on the string I was picking at and unraveled the very end of my sleeve.

Fuck.

Funny how one little string can tear apart so much. One little piece. It's always one little piece.

Dr. Forner was sitting across from me. We'd exchanged pleasantries when I first walked in, but there had been silence since. Being a couples therapist meant not taking sides, so talking to both parties, and neither separately, was essential. At least, that's the reasoning I came up with for his silence.

"Alright! Nice to see you, Avery!"

Dr. Forner's voice startled me and I looked up. Avery was

67

walking into the office, jacket in one hand, water bottle in another. A gallon jug. I rolled my eyes. He always had to be *that guy*. The gallon water jug guy. The tatted up, cigarette smoking guy. I loved that at first.

When did I stop loving that?

Avery sat down next to me, closer than usual. His jeans touched my leggings and I shimmied away quickly, getting as close to the armrest as I possibly could, making a gap of about an inch between us. But an inch was better than nothing. His t-shirt was a bit wet and so was his hair. He'd probably come from the gym and just gotten a shower before he got to therapy. Hence the wet hair and the lateness. Or he was with a girl and showered so I wouldn't smell her.

That's ridiculous.

Or is it?

"Crazy weather, isn't it? Last week it was in the 70s and now it's April and we're back in the 40s!"

Dr. Forner's attempt at small talk was well-intentioned but unsuccessful. Neither of us responded. I think I hoped that Avery would, and perhaps he thought that I would. Regardless, the statement fell flat, settling in a pool of awkwardness that seemed to swallow the entire room.

"Alright then," he said. "Let's dive right in."

I cleared my throat and went back to picking at the string on my sweater, watching the sleeve unravel more and more as I pulled.

"Odette, last week I asked you to tell me the moment you knew you had feelings for Avery. You've had some time to think about that away from –" he motioned around the room to signify *all this.* "Can you share what you remembered?"

I inhaled and wiped my sweaty palms on my leggings. They were black, now faded after years of wear. I had trouble buying new things. Except lingerie. For some reason.

Parker was the reason.

Everything else in my wardrobe was years old. I pulled my sweater down a bit to cover more of my thighs. It was teal and uncomfortably tight. I had chosen it quickly that morning with a "fuck this" attitude that meant not giving a damn if it looked good. The tightness was fine in the car, okay in the lobby, uncomfortable when I'd first entered Dr. Forner's office, and now it felt completely suffocating. I yanked at the folds of fabric that clung to my stomach.

This fucking shirt.

I could feel Avery and Dr. Forner looking at me.

"I remembered the time Avery drew all over his face with a pen. It was cute."

"Tell me more about that. How did you feel in that moment?"

I felt my lips form a slight smile completely on their own.

"It was cute. I thought he was really funny and sweet. He was trying to make me laugh. I don't know – it was just cute."

Dr. Forner smiled. "You two definitely had some fun moments at the beginning, and I'm sure since then. I know it'll be difficult but I want to talk a bit more about what Odette brought up in the session two weeks ago."

I could feel Avery shift uncomfortably next to me. I was sweating more, and I imagined he was, too.

"Can one of you start?"

I wondered if Avery would take the lead and, assuming he

wouldn't, I opened my mouth to start us off. But before I could begin, I heard him clear his throat.

"Odette and I started seeing each other when we were really young. She was 21 and I was 20."

I wanted to tell him he'd already told Dr. Forner that two weeks ago, but that would've been passive aggressive, and I was trying to work on that. So I let him continue, gently overlooking the redundancy, though it grated on me.

"She got pregnant three months after that," Avery said. "We ended up getting married when she was a couple months' pregnant. It felt like the best thing for everyone. I didn't have both my parents around when I was a kid."

I listened attentively, like a student soaking up the review before a big test.

"When she first got pregnant she wanted to get an abortion and I asked her not to. But she was never excited about the baby. The whole time she was just against it."

"That's not true," I said quietly, almost whispering.

"OK, Odette," Dr. Forner interjected calmly. "Let's wait for Avery to finish and you can express your feelings about what happened."

Avery continued, unphased. He told the story as if it were someone else's – emotionless, detached. Such a difference from the last session we'd discussed it.

"Odette was 31 weeks pregnant when the doctor said the baby didn't have a heartbeat. We named her Gracie when she was born."

I heard his voice crack at the end but I couldn't look at him.

Dr. Forner looked at me, his eyes reassuring me that it was my turn. As if this was a tennis match, only instead of hitting a ball we were hurtling words.

"I wanted to get an abortion *at first*. When I first found out. I was 21. We didn't have careers yet. We were so young. I just wanted to be a person before I was a mother." I paused, feeling the tears collect in my eyes, little puddles that made Dr. Forner look more like a pixelated cartoon than a human. "I *did* want her. Avery thinks I didn't want her and I don't know why because I did. *I* picked out her name. *I* painted the nursery. *I* bought the baby clothes."

"You *had* to do that. You didn't *want* to," Avery said, his jaw clenched in restraint. He wanted to yell, I could see that. But he wasn't. He was trying.

"I didn't *have* to do anything. Like you didn't *have* to sleep with that fucking girl."

Avery shot a surprised look at me. Six years and I'd never told him I knew. Six years.

"I didn't –"

"Oh don't play that game, Avery. I knew then. I knew every time you went to see her. I'm not stupid."

"It was six months. I ended it. I was wrong. I know that. I was hurt and angry. I'm ashamed of it now, and I was then."

I felt my mind go blank and then restart quickly, as if I was a system rebooting. I was surprised at how angry I felt, surprised that Avery admitted it so easily. Surprised I'd even said anything about it. Anger I thought was long gone seemed to boil inside of me, making every part of my core feel like it was burning. I wasn't just angry, though. Anger is such a casual term. I felt like the anger and bitterness and hurt and pain and regret and desperation and hopelessness I'd felt when Gracie died, and the months after, no longer had a haven in my body. They were free, escaping into the void space the two of us were wrapped in.

"Do you have any idea what it's like to lose your *child* and then, instead of having your husband *with* you, find out that he's sleeping with some fucking woman he met god knows where? To *know* that and not even say a fucking word. To feel the loss of *my* baby *alone*. Do you have any idea what that was like for me? How dare you tell me I didn't mourn my child. How dare you tell me I didn't *want* my child."

I collapsed into myself, wrapping my arms around my midsection like I was a little girl again, keeping myself from harm as best I could. But the harm had already been done.

Avery sighed, a long, heavy breath that cut through the momentary silence.

"It was six years ago. It was right after everything with Gracie. I was lost. I was hurt. Odette and I weren't talking. I was alone and – and I know it was wrong."

He was talking to Dr. Forner, looking past me, perhaps because admitting to an affair was easier when you didn't have to tell the one you were cheating on. He had started sobbing, little tears falling onto his jeans.

I fought to regain my composure, to look in some way strong.

"What about now?" I asked.

"What do you mean?

"What about *now?*"

"I'm not with anyone now. I swear. Odette, I swear."

"Where do you go at night? Where are you always going? You leave early and come home late every single day. Where are you going if you're not fucking somebody?"

Avery wiped his eyes and took my hand, squeezing it tight so I couldn't pull away. He knew me too well.

"Odette. I swear to you I'm not with anyone else. I haven't been home because it's been stressful and uncomfortable and I can't deal with it and I'm sorry for that. I'm sorry. I just drive around. Sometimes I go to the mall and walk around before they close. Sometimes I just drive. But I'm *not* with anyone else. I wouldn't do that to you again."

The last sentence ripped through my heart like it was paper.

He's lying. He's probably lying. And even if he isn't. he did it before. Being with Parker isn't the same thing. Avery did it first. He did it first.

He did it first.

Dr. Forner cleared his throat.

"It seems like there's a lot of broken trust here on both sides. Avery, do you believe Odette when she says she wanted the baby?"

Circling back to Gracie hit me hard. It was the one topic I didn't want to discuss. I'd talk about Avery's infidelity all day. But not this.

"I…I do. I do."

"You didn't for seven years and now you do?" I questioned.

"We've never talked about it before."

Maybe all he needed all along was to hear me say that I'd wanted her. He was right, we'd never discussed it. The day we buried her was the last we'd talked about it. And for six years, we'd lived our lives, happy moments and sad moments, but always somewhat removed – always with a well between us. And then, almost a year to the day before our first counseling session, I'd asked if he wanted to try for a baby. And it was like that one question started a domino effect. All the things we hadn't said came pouring onto us like ash from a volcano. Not at first, not right then and there. But after, and for months. We argued; we yelled at each other for all the things that didn't matter, but we never once mentioned Gracie. She was a hurt that went too deep to discuss. So we yelled about his job not making enough and our house not being big enough, and my job being too physically demanding, and he said maybe I wouldn't make a good mother because I'm too selfish and then we stopped yelling and we stopped arguing and we stopped talking. And he moved to the couch and I took the bed. And then one day, two months before Parker was transferred to my shift – two months before I realized what it meant to be loved and nurtured and needed and wanted – he suggested we try counseling. And I said OK. And there we were, talking about the one thing neither of us wanted to deal with. Putting our hands on the burning embers of a fire that had burned far, far too long between us. In that moment, I felt closer to him than I'd felt in years. And I felt more pain than I had since Gracie.

He held me as I broke down, the two of us crying in each other's arms as Dr. Forner sat in front of us, telling us it was okay to show our feelings, to comfort one another, to express our pain.

"It's okay to be vulnerable with one another," he said. "I'm going to give you the room for a minute so you can have a moment together."

He walked out and I put my head on Avery's lap, letting him stroke my hair and the side of my face as we both cried. I felt like someone had opened a dam and my tears were unstoppable. No force could halt them or contain them. But that was okay. Crying over Gracie, over the lives we wanted, over the dreams we had, and the anger we'd let fester for so long, that was okay. At least in that moment, for those minutes alone, we could be us again. The us we were before everything. We could take a long, slow, painful ride back through time and revisit the little homes we'd made and burned over time, and we could live inside them again, just for a while. For those moments together, those homes were ours again.

CHAPTER

SIX

———

I SAT ON THE FLOOR OF THE BATHROOM at home with my eyes closed, music playing through air pods that seemed more connected to my soul than my ears. Some people say music is their refuge. For me, music is my skin, the boundary that separates and contains. It embodies everything inside me. Without it, I would, in every way, disintegrate.

Foolishly, I thought our session would follow through into our daily lives, but it hadn't. Sometimes I imagined our life like a movie. And, in a movie, that would've been the romantic end. Avery and I would've found each other again in that moment and, in a way, we had. But that's just what it was – a moment. I wanted to think he believed that Gracie's death wasn't my fault. Just like, I think, he wanted to believe that I thought he was telling the truth about his affair being long since over. But the *real* truth was, we wanted to believe each other because the moment was raw and real, not because we actually did. And when the proverbial dust settled and the clouds broke apart, the sun shone on the same divide that had kept us apart for years before.

It's like breaking open an old scar. Air can soothe it for a short time, but then, as it heals, it begins to itch. And the more you scratch it, the worse it feels, and the longer it takes to heal. We'd opened a wound that day, and at first it felt comforting. But the comfort didn't last. That same afternoon, Avery texted me to tell me he would be leaving for a few days. Apparently he'd already packed bags and set them in the car, so he'd be leaving straight from work. We didn't have time to settle back into the routine – to see if the scab would begin to fester again. Avery didn't let it have air. He poured some vinegar on it and patched it up with a band aid. And promptly left.

I didn't ask where Avery was going, or how long he'd be gone. Somehow, in a completely surreal way, those types of inquiries seemed too personal. Whatever he had planned was his.

There, some hours after he texted me, around when he should've been getting off work and departing to god knows where – I sat there, listening, or more accurately absorbing music, my mind both completely full and completely blank at the same time. Our brains are such paradoxes, aren't they? It's as if you can have racing thoughts with thoughts that don't exist. How can that be? A jumble of nothingness. A mess that is a void. The songs changed in turn, but I didn't notice. I was just existing. Leo had his head resting on my lap, and Camden was off somewhere, probably keeping tabs on the food dish I hadn't filled yet. The faucet was dripping, making a funny *glurp* sound as the water hit the basin, and I could hear it through the low music on my air pods. The leak was slow, almost like the drops were suspended in the air for a spell before falling into the sink. And, for some odd reason, it reminded me of the day Bridgett told me my mother had died. I remembered hearing her say the words but all I could focus on was the sound of the kitchen sink, left on just a bit from when I'd finished the dishes a few minutes earlier. I'd been alone at home, which wasn't uncommon at the time. Bridgett spent most of her hours off work at the hospital with our mom and I "tended house," as she used to say, which she made out to be an extremely important task that, I realized later, was her way of distracting me from seeing our mother's deteriorating health. I could so vividly see that moment that Bridgett came home, her eyes swollen and cheeks damp. She ran to me almost instantly, flinging her signature 2000s backpack purse to the side of the room so it hit the couch next to the front door and fell to the floor beside it. You can tell when someone is going to deliver news like that. Even as a little kid, you can tell. But when she knelt down to get closer to my level and put her hands on my shoulders gently, looking tenderly into my eyes, all I could pay attention to was the *plip plip plip* from the faucet, signaling that I'd messed up the one responsibility I had. Our mom had always reminded me to turn off the faucet because the little finicky tap was always catching back on after you turned it off. "Odette! The FAUCET!" she used to yell from across the house, somehow capable of hearing it drip from rooms away.

Leaning against the floor of the bathroom, listening to the faucet sing its song of defeat, and my air pods play a song I'd never heard before, I remembered that look in Bridgett's eyes and the similar sound from years before. I could've gotten up and nudged the handle just a touch to close it, but somehow, a part of me liked the connection to that memory, even though it was painful. Because it brought me back to a time right before I knew what loss was like -- moments before I understood that life takes so much more than it gives.

I let myself get lost in my mind – so lost that the sound of my phone ringing made my entire body jump. My eyes jolted themselves open. I'd considered putting it on airplane mode earlier, but I'd decided against it. *Just in case.* Just in case what? Avery calls and says he's stuck in a ditch somewhere and needs me, and only me, to come help him? Parker calls and says he's ready for another visit? Impossible. Avery was entirely self-sufficient and Parker was still several hours away in another state with another woman *or was I the other woman* so there wasn't much reason to babysit the phone.

But the call wasn't from Avery or Parker. It was Bridgett. I considered declining. I wasn't in any mood for small talk or to listen to her talk endlessly about my two nieces, though I loved them to death. But I couldn't ignore her.

"Hey, Bridge."

I tried to sound remotely cheerful. It came out flat. My mind was stuck half in the present and half in the past, and neither one was desirous of conversation. Luckily, Bridgett was never one to pick up on subtle things like mannerisms or gestures or intonation.

"Hey! I was wondering if you wanted me and the girls to come up tomorrow?"

I'd worked the same shift for the last five years – the same two days off, one day on – yet she could never remember which days I was free and which ones I wasn't.

"Working tomorrow," I said, somewhat curtly.

My sister and I had a delicate relationship. She was 10 years older than me, and the age gap between us was often incredibly apparent. She'd had two daughters from her first marriage to a man named Tim, who I never liked and truthfully, I think, neither did she. They divorced when the girls were 2 and 3 and, to my knowledge, she hadn't seen him since. She was a single mother for all of a year before marrying Skylar, a tall, incredibly muscular man who owned a brewery and possibly drank more than he served. But he was a good guy. He was never a harmful drunk or a belligerent drunk. He was just drunk. When he was sober, he was incredibly present, caring for the girls like they were his own. It was, honestly, beautiful to see. He would go through bouts – a year of heavy drinking; six months of sobriety; six months of drinking; a year of sobriety. Currently, he was in a sober phase, and Bridgett seemed to be soaking it in, enjoying every last drop of attentiveness he gave her.

I saw the girls far less than I wanted. They were seven hours away by car and the idea of driving that was never something Avery was interested in doing and, for some reason, I felt odd going alone – even to my own sister. Avery was my buffer. He allowed for couples conversation, rather than the one-on-one with my sister that usually led to questions about when we would be trying again for another baby, and when I was going to get a more "practical" job. I hadn't told her anything about my problems with Avery – ever, actually. Nor had I mentioned Parker. There are some things you don't bring up to family, or anyone.

I could hear Bridgett sigh on the other end.

"But it's Josie's birthday."

"I know. I sent a gift. Didn't you get it yet?"

Josie was turning the big 1-0, and I did want to see her for it, despite the inherent pain that comes from seeing children you're related to reach milestones yours will never see.

"We did get it. She's going to open it on her birthday. She said she's very excited."

"That's good – I think she'll like it."

"Well can you take off or something? She really wants to see you."

I rubbed my temples, preparing for the headache the conversation was already giving me.

"Bridge, I'm working tomorrow and it's too late to take off. Can you come up next week? Avery's on a work trip *whatever work he's doing is beyond me* but he'll be back by then."

In truth, I had no idea when Avery would be back, but I had no other excuse to postpone. Seeing her – seeing the girls – in light of everything, the last therapy session, the dredging up of every past hurt, including Gracie – I just couldn't do it.

"Okay. Will you let me know a date?"

"Absolutely. Can you put Jenna and Josie on the phone so I can say hi?"

"You're on speaker, Aunt Odie."

I loved that name. I was Aunt Odie to two perfect little girls and I was eternally grateful for that. Beyond them, I didn't have a title. I was supposed to, but I didn't. Being an aunt was like being gifted a stolen jewel. It was a beautiful gesture and it felt amazing to have, but it wasn't mine. And it never would be.

I listened to the girls chatter about school and slime and pizza parties and slumber parties and all other kinds of parties little girls have for at least half an hour. I don't think I stopped smiling the whole time.

"I'll call you tomorrow, OK?"

I heard Jenna say "OK" really loudly, followed by Josie quietly admonishing her.

"She was talking to ME. It's MY birthday tomorrow."

"I was talking to both of you," I interjected. "I'll talk to BOTH OF YOU tomorrow. Happy early birthday, Josie."

I expected to talk to Bridgett again but one of the girls hung up. I wondered when Avery would be back. Would he even make it to the next therapy session? Some fucked up part of me wanted him to stay gone for a while. So I could come home to an empty house. Not empty of him, necessarily, but void of the thick, foul odor of futility that seemed to blanket the air when we were together. I wanted time alone. I wanted time with Parker, even though I knew it couldn't be at home.

Tomorrow would be my last shift without Parker. He would be back Sunday, and back to work on Tuesday. What was funny about missing Parker was that I knew I'd be greeted with one of two versions of him: The Parker who had spent seven days with his wife and desperately needed a break *aka me* or The Parker who had spent seven days with his wife and now felt guilty for sleeping with me. I hoped – prayed – it would be the former. I needed him. I needed the comfort of his hands, the well of support from his warm, welcoming body – to feel wanted again.

To be Lucy.

CHAPTER

SEVEN

B y the time Tuesday rolled around, I still hadn't heard from Avery. No text. No phone call. No letter. No note affixed to an unwilling pigeon. Nothing. Our next therapy session was scheduled for that Thursday, and I questioned if he'd even show up. Or if he'd put in enough notice at work for this impromptu hiatus from normal life.

I woke up at 4:30 as I always did. Rolled out of bed. Fed the dogs. Left instructions for the dogsitter – the neighbor's 17-year-old daughter who, although an honor student, consistently forgot how much kibble they each got unless I reminded her. I always showered the night before a shift, just to cut down on time in the morning. All I had to do for myself was get dressed (which usually meant PT clothes) and put a dab of eye shadow on each eyelid and call it a day. But today was different. Parker was coming back.

I put on my uniform, but not before slipping on the red bra he liked and the matching red lace panties, the ensemble he'd asked to see some shifts before. I figured I'd surprise him. At the same time, I tried to steel myself for the possibility he'd want nothing to do with me. That he would have changed his mind about me

– however his mind had been before – in the time he was gone. I told myself I would be ready for either eventuality. But I wasn't. Not in the slightest. I wanted nothing more than to be the center of his world again, if ever I was.

I wasn't.

I couldn't be.

But I wanted to feel like I was.

Is that so wrong?

I put a little more makeup on than usual, sticking with nudes but adding a little pop of mascara and a gentle swipe of black eye liner. And a modest, shimmering lip balm for good measure.

Two pats each on Leo and Camden's heads, and a little boop on each nose, and I was on my way.

I walked in around 5 a.m. and loaded my gear on the ambulance. I was taking inventory when I heard his voice, sharing a conversation with Daws, or so it sounded from across the bay. I always thought Parker's voice was incredibly comforting. He had this musical way of talking – not like he was singing, really, but that the words just seemed to flow so easily through him. He never seemed to struggle with what to say or how to say it. Everything seemed to just come naturally to him. I felt my heart start beating just a little faster and I closed my eyes.

Don't be stupid. Don't be stupid. Don't be stupid.

I imagined myself walking over to him and tripping over the aid bag on the bay floor, or trying to tell a joke and fumbling my words, or saying hello too loudly or too excitedly in front of everyone and garnering weird looks and suspicious whispers.

For some reason, my mind brought me back to the night of my junior prom, when a boy named Addison was supposed to pick up. I set up in a chair right next to the window that had the best view of the driveway. And there I waited. I waited through sweaty hands and quick-moving blood that seemed to settle in my stomach and feed the dancing butterflies that held court there. I waited through the cooling off of my sweaty hands, and the nausea of rejection that replaced the sickness of anticipation. I waited and waited and waited. And then, after an hour, he showed up. His hair was spiked with gel and a single small loop earring adorned his right ear. He had a suit on, but the dress shirt under his jacket was untucked. Like he was making an effort for the show of it, and making a statement for the record.

"I don't think this boy is good for her," I heard Bridgett say on the phone to god-knows-who in the living room as Addison opened the front door without knocking.

But I didn't care. In just a few minutes, I'd forgotten that he was an hour late. Or that he didn't bring me flowers or take me to dinner. I was just grateful to be in his orbit. I didn't care who I was to him, as long as I was *something* to him. First loves are such tricky things. We know so little about ourselves when we dive into the arms of that first safe haven – that first person to ignite something within us that begs to be set free. If we're lucky, those arms belong to someone who desires us for us, and not for the mask we wear when the sunlight shines too brightly on our secrets. But most of the time, our first love doesn't deserve the huge piece of us we give them. As I sat alone at a table that night at prom, watching Addison dance with Fretta Wilson, I knew I'd given my heart to the wrong person. But I was in every way powerless to get it back.

Parker's voice got louder as he walked toward me, and I stirred, knocking myself out of that memory I hadn't thought of in years. But, in hindsight, I suppose first loves and stolen loves are very much the same. Both feel so perfect when you fall into them, and neither are meant to last. They're not yours to have.

"Well if it isn't Firefighter Lucille Carrigan."

I looked up and saw Parker, grinning widely as he looked at me.

"Lieutenant." I tried not to smile, but my excitement gave me away immediately.

He motioned for me to join him upstairs, waving his hand toward the door and nodding in the same direction, as if one cue wasn't enough. I nodded and waited for him to walk up first.

He was standing in the office when I walked up a few moments later, and beckoned impatiently for me to come in.

"Close the door," he said as I move toward him.

As soon as I did, he put his arms around my waist and picked me up. He kissed me – more passionately than he ever had – faster, dirtier, more sexual than sensual. Usually, his kisses were passionate in their tenderness, slower, and unhurried, as if ours was the last kiss ever to be experienced by anyone, and we were savoring it all for ourselves. But this time, it was a kiss of craving. A kiss of longing. A kiss that said he wanted every part of me. He started pulling my tucked in shirt out of my pants and I gently put my hand on his to stop him. I looked at him in his eyes, a look that said *not here* and he nodded in affirmation. He put me down and I straightened my uniform.

"Miss me?" I said, laughing.

"Just a bit, Lucy. Miss me?"

"Nah."

I considered asking how his trip was, but judging by the reception he gave me, I assumed it didn't go well. I didn't want to know things were bad between him and his wife. I didn't want them to be. I had no ill feelings toward her. I didn't wish for her to die or disappear or get hit by a meteor in some freak stroke of nature. But I didn't want to know if things went poorly, because I didn't want to feel like in some way I was stealing him away, even if I was. Our love didn't exist in this world. It existed outside of the realities of normal life. Or so I wanted to believe. It didn't matter who we were with outside of one another, because we weren't in their orbit. We were in a galaxy all our own. It was separate. It had to be.

I opened the door, smiled at Parker, and walked out. He was back.

He was back.

◆ ◆ ◆

I was laying in my bunk scrolling through Facebook when Avery texted me. It was a little after 10 p.m. and most everyone was settled in for the night, anxiously awaiting a fire that probably wouldn't happen, but that we hoped for just the same.

"Back."

I stared at his text for a solid minute, considering a myriad of responses.

Thanks for telling me you're back. Now how about telling me where you were?

Who was she?

How was your trip away from the realities of our crumbling marriage?

You fucking dick.

They got more aggressive the more I thought about them so I settled on "OK."

"Jess fed Leo and Camden," I wrote, somewhat wanting to extend the conversation to see if he'd share anything.

"OK."

He kept typing, then stopping, then typing, then stopping, little bubbles dancing on the screen over and over again with little intermissions. But he didn't say anything else.

So much for communication.

I considered asking him about having my nieces over. But I didn't. What was the point? He'd say no anyway. Plus, it was hardly the right time to entertain anyone, even if it was my own family.

I'll make some excuse.

My phone vibrated and I looked at the screen to see a message from Parker. He was texting me from two bunks over.

"You looked hot as fuck today, Lucy."

I smiled.

"Thank you, Parker."

"Meet in the office at 2300?"

"Sure."

I settled in to what I hoped would be a slow EMS night and put Casablanca on my phone while I waited to talk to Parker in the office. Every shift I tried to watch that movie and every shift I seemed to get through the first 10 minutes before getting a call. I'd probably seen those 10 minutes about 100 times. But it was like a tradition. Just like the office visits. Both gave me a sense of comfort, if only for a while.

◆ ◆ ◆

We never planned to have sex. We didn't set specific occasions for rendezvous like that. We did set times for hanging out, for seeing each other alone. And when I went into the office at 2300, I wasn't expecting to do anything other than talk, despite how excited he'd been to see me earlier in the day. But I was somewhat hoping. I always hoped for more than talking. I didn't get him for days or weeks or special occasions or holidays. I didn't get him for those moments that define a couple. I got him for scattered moments, little here and there, in-between times. So, naturally, I wanted to make the most of each of them.

"Have a good day?"

His voice was cheerful but a little subdued, like he was sitting on a secret he couldn't wait to tell me, but dreaded revealing at the same time.

I nodded. "You ok?"

"Yeah, yeah, fine. Sit with me?"

I sat down across from him, the desk posing a convenient buffer for any activities either of us might have been imagining. He held out his hand and I welcomed it with mine.

"You sure you're OK? You seem off?"

"You got that from four words?"

"I know you, remember?"

He laughed. "I remember."

"So…"

"So?"

"So what is it?"

He took off his hat and rubbed his head, bringing his thumb

and forefinger to his temples and letting them sit there, as if protecting his eyes from something he couldn't bring himself to see.

"Parker?"

"My wife wants to try for a baby."

I stared at him, completely aware that my mouth was open, and utterly unable to do anything to ameliorate the embarrassingly shocked look on my face.

I must have been silent for a while, because I suddenly heard him say "Lucy," and I jolted back to reality. In however many seconds passed between his statement and his exclamation of my name, I don't think I had a single thought. I had a litany of emotions, but zero thoughts. It felt like my blood had been replaced with coolant. Everything inside me got really, really cold. And then hot. Really fucking hot. Oddly enough, I didn't necessarily think of Gracie -- but the pain I felt when I held her tiny, unbreathing body in my arms the day she was born, that feeling surged through me like a shark after its prey. I hadn't been expecting it, so I was, in every way, defenseless against it. It wasn't that he was having a baby. It was that I didn't have mine. Or maybe it was that he was having a baby. Maybe it was that he was having a baby with his wife and I had no baby with my husband. Maybe it was because their marriage was still fine and mine was falling apart. Maybe it was jealousy or heartbreak or fear of losing him. A child changes things. For both parties.

"What did you tell her," I asked finally.

"I told her I don't want to."

"Is that how you really feel?"

"I mean, I don't want kids. She knew that going in."

"Things change."

"This doesn't change."

"You should think about it." I heard myself say those words, rather than mindfully saying them. I was, in a way, once again advocating for her, someone I didn't know, who I was knowingly screwing over, simply because I felt an odd sense of responsibility to protect her.

"Why?"

"Because it's important for a woman to have kids if she wants to. It's important to be a mother if you can."

He looked at me, seemingly realizing for the first time in the conversation that this topic was a difficult one for me.

"Lucy, I'm sorry. I –"

"It's ok. Really."

"I don't want to have kids and then resent them, or resent her. I just don't want kids. Is that wrong?"

"No, Parker. That's not wrong."

"Tell her that," he said, laughing, an awkward joke that fell short of being funny and just landed in the territory of uncomfortable silence.

"Do me a favor, OK?"

"Sure. Anything."

"Don't talk to me about you guys wanting to have kids. If she ends up getting pregnant, tell me. Otherwise, I don't want to know."

He looked at me, his eyes a little hurt and a little surprised. We could talk about anything with each other generally. So this new rule was probably somewhat disconcerting for him. But I needed it to be there. I needed boundaries, however fucked up they were.

"OK. Sure. Sorry."

"No, it's fine. Really. I just can't talk about that. Y'know?"

"Yeah."

He didn't. He couldn't. But he tried to.

We sat in silence for a few more minutes until he stood up abruptly and walked to a little bookbag in the corner of the room. He pulled out a throw blanket that looked way too big to fit in there, and I wondered for a second if this would be some sort of magic trick. He laid it on the floor and sat down, motioning for me to take a place next to him. He propped up against the wall and I lay down next to him, resting my head on his lap. He curled the end of the blanket up so it covered my legs, sandwiching me comfortably between two halves of blanket. It was uncomfortable against the hard wood floor, but cozy at the same time. He gently placed his hand on my head and rested his head against the wall. We didn't say anything, and he didn't try to do anything other than just exist with me in that moment. And I was OK with that. Closeness comes in many forms, and sometimes being held by someone can be more intimate than sleeping with them.

"I won't bring it up again," he said after some time had passed. And he didn't. Not once.

SESSION
FIVE

———

AVERY SAT NEXT TO ME AND PUT HIS HAND on my knee. Dr. Forner caught onto it just as quickly as I did, but for different reasons. He seemed happy about the unusual affection; I was bewildered.

Avery hadn't said a word to me since coming back. By the time I got home from Tuesday's shift, he'd already left for work. I imagined there'd be roses and a note laying on the counter – little machinations of my mind that romanticized relationships far outside and beyond what they ever were in reality. And, unsurprisingly, there weren't any flowers waiting for me. There was just a dirty plate with remnants of eggs and toast Avery had left behind on the counter, waiting for me to pick up.

"How have things been since the last time we met?" Dr. Forner asked, clicking his pen slowly and methodically, as if it, too, were contemplating our relationship.

"Good, I think," Avery responded quickly.

I shot a look at him – one that probably looked half-confused, half-angry.

"Good?"

"I mean. Not good. I went on a trip just to clear my head. Just to get away. But things haven't been bad, is what I meant. We haven't argued."

"We haven't argued because we haven't talked."

"Still."

"Okay," Dr. Forner interjected. "Avery, what prompted your getaway?"

"I just need to clear my head. Like I said"

"Did you tell Odette you were leaving beforehand?"

I wondered how he knew that Avery'd sprung it on me. He always seemed so intuitive. That was something I liked about him.

"I told her right before I left."

"Avery," he started, before quickly adding "and Odette." He obviously didn't want to point admonishment in one direction over another. This was couples counseling, where the battlefield is always fair and no one is ever really wrong, or right. "No relation-ship – no marriage – can work if either partner feels the need to leave to resolve problems. You solve problems together. Now, that being said, if one of you needs space, a few deep breaths in another room can be beneficial to avoid heated arguments." He took a deep breath, as if to give us an example of what he meant. "But overnight trips – weekend trips – anything extended doesn't help your relationship thrive. It just shows the other person you're not willing to try, and that you're avoidant. Does that make sense?"

I nodded.

Well I wasn't the one to leave, he was. Tell him *that.*

"Yes," Avery responded.

I shook my knee a little to signify I wanted Avery to remove his hand, and he did.

"Guys, let's go back aways. We talked a lot about Gracie and the trauma surrounding that. Can you tell me how you dealt with that at the time?"

Other than Avery cheating on me? Let's see…

"We didn't, really," I said. "We talked about it at the hospital when I had Gracie. But we didn't bring it up after that."

"That's interesting. That's a big thing to happen for you to not discuss, don't you think?"

"We discussed it at the hospital, like Odette said, but it just wasn't something we talked about after that," Avery said. "It was a lot to handle. I think we handled it fine separately."

"I don't know that I agree," Dr. Forner said. "Because you're here. And, from what I can tell, a lot of the struggle you're dealing with now stems from that trauma and the microtraumas that occurred around it and because of it."

He paused a moment, not long enough for either of us to respond, but just long enough for his words to settle in the air.

"You mentioned a few sessions ago, Odette, that you brought up having another baby and that triggered an emotional response from Avery. Which, you said, was the impetus for you both seeking therapy."

I nodded.

"Can you share what his reaction meant to you?"

I felt squeamish, uneasy. Remembering that day felt like thinking about the beginning of the end. And yet, in a way, I think we'd been over the day we came home from the hospital, a family of two instead if three. I remember cooking dinner – garlic chicken and cooked carrots. And mashed potatoes. I remember mashing the potatoes. It's so weird what sticks in your mind. Other details fall away – like what I was wearing or the weather that day – but I remember mashing the potatoes. Avery was sitting on the couch half-watching TV, half putzing around on his phone. A baby came on the screen – some commercial for a new nursing bra -- and, for the first time in years, I felt a little swelling of excitement before the familiar feeling of grief. And, without thinking, I blurted out, "I think we should try for another baby."

Avery just looked at me then. And, with a look that seemed almost like one of betrayal, he said a firm, "No" and walked into the bedroom. And that was that. Neither of us had mentioned it since.

"And how did that make you feel?" Dr. Forner asked after I related the incident.

"Rejected. Hurt. Like he didn't want me."

Like he didn't want any of it. Like our lives meant nothing. Like I meant nothing.

"And since then, what happened that prompted you to want therapy?" Dr. Forner asked. "That was your idea, right, Avery?"

"We haven't slept in the same bed in…months."

Try years.

"We don't act like a married couple. We're completely separate."

"Do you remember when that separation started? Was it after that discussion?"

I paused to think.

"We didn't sleep together a lot after Gracie died," I said. "Occasionally. We did things together; we did have good things happen. It wasn't all bad."

I stopped, realizing I hadn't answered the question in the slightest.

"It really got bad after that, I think. We pretty much stopped talking altogether."

I looked over to see Avery sobbing quietly into his hands, and I felt an instant pang of guilt like a whip piercing against my stomach.

"I want my marriage back," he said, clearing his throat in a transparent attempt to hide his broken voice, "I want my wife back."

Something about the way he said that, equal parts genuine and vulnerable, struck me hard in my core. I was surprised by my thoughts then. I wanted so badly to want Avery. And, in a way, I did. But I wanted the Avery from before. I wanted the love we had before we lost it. And, as fucked up as it was, I wanted Avery to find his own version of Parker – someone who would be gentle with him and kind to him and accepting of every little quirk and idiosyncrasy he had. Avery and I weren't like that anymore. I couldn't peel off the layers of hurt and start over with clean, unblemished skin. What was done was done. We weren't just broken; we were shattered.

I remembered then a little analogy Bridgett used to tell me when I was a teen sneaking out at 2 a.m. to drive around with my friends. We never did anything besides drive, but her maternal instinct was strong, and her desire to be able to feel like she could trust me was just as robust. Being a sister turned mother in a short time can do that. I didn't understand then, but I did as an adult. And then, after Gracie, even though I didn't get to keep her, I understood even more. She used to say, "Odette, trust is like a vase. If you break it, you can try to put it back together, but it will never be the same as it was before. It will forever be broken.

It might be patched up and it could even hold flowers and water again. But it will never be what it was before. It will never be unbroken."

It occurred to me in that moment, sitting with Avery and Dr. Forner in the little office that only seemed to get smaller and smaller every time we were there, that the two of us were just like a broken vase. We could put glue on the cracks and try to fit the pieces back together, but it would never be whole again. It would never be the way it was. It would always be broken. Avery didn't want *this* wife back. He wanted the woman he had before, the woman who existed before Gracie, before the affair, before the arguments, before the tears. He wanted someone unscarred. And that was entirely impossible to give him.

"What can the two of you do this week to strengthen your marriage?" Dr. Forner asked, turning to his legal pad and writing a few notes that looked more like a jumble of letters than real words.

Neither of us said anything. To strengthen something means it already has some sort of foundation to begin with. We didn't. Our ships, separate as ever, were sinking.

"How about a date night? Can you do something together?"

We looked at each other and, for the first time in a very, very long time, it felt like both of us were thinking the same thing.

Jesus Christ that sounds miserable.

Neither of us wanted to push ourselves into uncomfortable, forced togetherness.

Silence.

"Do you want to work on your marriage?"

Dr. Forner's question was pointed, and a little bit harsh, as if he was calling us out. In a way, that's exactly what he was doing.

I looked down at my hands and began nervously picking off my red nail polish. I'd put it on for Parker's first day back and now, having served its purpose, I no longer had need for it. Wearing nail polish made me feel unnaturally feminine. I didn't like it. I guess Avery nodded, because Dr. Forner said "that's good," followed by "pick one night this week and do something just the two of you."

What was funny was that, had Avery not said anything, I don't think I would have either. I wanted to want to work on the marriage. But I didn't. I just wanted to be done. I was so, so ready to be done.

CHAPTER

EIGHT

———

"A, B, D and E."

It was a little game Parker and I played during our office time at the station. I'd show him one of those Instagram "pick one" graphics, usually donut flavors or dessert varieties, and he'd have to pick which ones I would go for first. And then I'd pick for him. It never ceased to amaze me how spot on we always were for each other.

"Yes!" I said, sounding more excited than I probably should have.

"I know you, doll," he said, turning back to his computer screen to finish the last of the reports for the evening, unless/until another call came in. I loved when he called me that. I loved the idea that I had a place in his heart that warranted a pet name. "Lucy" was cute, but "doll" was endearing. It said that I meant something.

"OK, my turn," I said. "A, B, C and F."

He studied the graphic intently, taking in the different options. In this case, we were looking at a healthy selection of muffins. Blueberry, coffee cake, chocolate chip, peanut butter, banana, chocolate banana, and a few others.

"Yes…yes…yes…and yes."

"I know you, Parker," I said, mocking him just a little. I playfully flipped his baseball cap off and he laughed, reaching down to pick it up without breaking eye contact. He knew he could make me laugh with just a look. I loved that about him.

"You really are incredible, you know that?"

I wasn't used to his kind of compliments. I wasn't really used to any compliments. But his were so incredibly sweet. They made me uncomfortable, truthfully. I didn't know how to accept them gracefully, so I usually just laughed or played them off with a self-deprecating joke.

It was the middle of a slow day at the station, so we were more careful than usual. Our voices were lowered and our chairs set a few feet apart, rather than side by side.

"How're things on the home front?" he asked.

The question was unusual. He talked about his wife occasionally, which never ceased to frustrate me, but I rarely mentioned Avery. It felt unnatural to talk to my lover about my husband. Having an affair was bad enough. Keeping the worlds as separate as possible was a necessity.

"What do you mean?"

"Well I know they aren't great."

"Yeah. We're in couples therapy. Fun stuff."

I hoped my brevity would signal that I didn't want to talk about it, but it seemed that he did.

"I get it. Sometimes I wish I never got married."

"Oh?"

"Yeah. I mean I love my wife. But it's just not…"

"Not what?"

"I don't know. Sometimes it just doesn't feel right. We get along fine. I don't have any glaring issues. But there's just no spark, y'know? There's no –" he made a hand motion at his chest to signify "fire" or "passion."

"Yeah. Same boat."

Only it wasn't, really. There were glaring issues in my marriage. Lack of spark was the least of our concerns.

"You're different."

"What do you mean?"

"I mean you're different. I've never felt this way about anyone before."

I didn't know what to say.

"Maybe you guys just need to work on things. Try counseling. Sometimes couples lose that after being together a while."

There I was again, making an odd attempt to help him save something I didn't want him to be in in the first place.

"Maybe," he said. "Or maybe it just isn't right anymore."

I didn't know what to say. Again. I wanted him to be mine, but I didn't want to be the reason he wasn't hers. And the idea of him going through what I was with Avery made my heart hurt. I loved Parker too much to push him toward that kind of pain.

"It'll be okay, Parker."

I smiled at him sweetly and made a little heart symbol with my hands. He laughed and returned it.

"You're the best," he mouthed silently.

You are. More than you know.

◆ ◆ ◆

The day after shift was a Saturday, and Avery and I had decided to see a movie. It probably wouldn't pass The Dr. Forner Test of Intimacy, but it was something. And it was, to us, better than nothing. We'd gone back and forth on what to do, sharing ideas like bowling (too crowded on a Saturday), mini golf (too cold), dinner (couldn't decide on a place), drinks (too expensive), and the mall (we're not teenagers) before he suggested a movie and, in an effort to avoid further discussion, I immediately agreed. He picked the movie. To my surprise, he picked a romance, a period picture about a man and woman finding love at the height of the second World War. With several action flicks to choose from, I was shocked he landed on that one. It struck me as sweet. A little olive branch. He was thinking about me. He was making a choice with me in mind. It was different, but it was nice. We got popcorn and sodas and a bag of M&M's and laughed during the previews about the irony of paying $30 for food at the theater plus ticket cost when we thought drinks would be too expensive. He held the popcorn in his lap and I poured the M&M's in to create a little mixture we always used to share together. That had been our cinema tradition what felt like forever ago. There was so much anger that held space between us, but there was so much love. Even then. Even after everything, there was love. He was a part of me. Even when we were fighting; even when we weren't speaking — in the worst of times, he was still the cornerstone of my world. I'd tried so hard to fence off that part of myself — that love I held for him -- for so long. We had lost ourselves in our marriage, but in some eternal way, we'd never completely lost one another.

He put his arm around me and it felt foreign, like a stranger getting awkwardly close to me. But, after a minute or two, the familiarity began to creep back in, and the warmth of his body settled into mine.

I cried when the movie ended. It was a corny film, stunningly saccharine and insanely cliché, but at the end, the two main characters decided to live separately, to leave their love behind so that the woman could save her children. She abandoned him to save them. I related to her. I felt like I'd left Avery behind when I lost Gracie. My mind connected dots from the movie's conclusion to my own experiences in a way that, to most people, would probably make no sense. But to me, in that moment, I was Marian in 1941, choosing to leave the love of her life to save her two daughters. I felt what she felt. I sobbed softly into Avery's black and white checkered flannel, and I felt his hand reach up to his face to wipe away a few tears of his own. We both felt it. We read far too much into the movie than we probably should have. But, as with all art, you give it meaning, not the other way around.

I hadn't felt that close to Avery in years. We held hands as we walked back to the car, neither of us saying anything, because we didn't have to. There was beauty in that silence. There was forgiveness in it. And, when we went to sleep, we slept in the same bed, nestled together for the first time in so very long. He kissed my forehead as I fell asleep and as he did, I felt a kind of peace I hadn't expected or prepared for. I realized, then, that there was familiar love and there was passionate love. There was the love for someone your heart knows, and the love for someone it wants. I knew Avery; I wanted Parker. And knowing that, feeling that as he held me, cut into my heart like a hot knife.

SESSION

SIX

———

AVERY SMILED AT ME. FOR THE FIRST TIME in years, his smile made me feel warm. Like he was soothing me from the inside. We'd just finished the usual pleasantries that started off every therapy session. The *loving this weather lately* and *pretty soon we'll be able to get rid of these jackets!* that all seemed to be variations on the same theme. Which was, quite obviously, the therapist's known best practice of Making the Client Feel at Ease Before a Session by Beginning with Small Talk and Not Jumping Right into Trauma History. It was never successful, but never avoided either.

Avery's smile was reassuring. It wasn't one of passion – more of empathy. This was a road we were travelling together. For better or worse. One way or another.

"Let's dive right in then, shall we?"

The sunlight hit the window and pelted down on my side of the couch. It was just hot enough to warm me a bit. I'd taken off my jacket with no desire to do the work of putting it back on, but I was chilly in a short sleeve t-shirt. The sun's timing and intensity couldn't have been better.

"That date night we talked about last session. What did you

pick to do and how did it go?"

I looked at Avery and smiled. The memory of it was nice. It felt like a warm blanket on the day of the first snow of the year. It was a little stake in the road, a place to come back to when we were lost. And we were always getting lost. Maybe that was our version of natural. Maybe that's just how we were meant to be.

"It was nice," I said, nervously tucking a stray hair behind my ears. I caught a glimpse of the fading caramel highlights and remembered I never should've strayed from my natural brown. At least that's reversible. It was a decision I'd made a couple of months back, on a whim – a day off and an empty schedule means many things can happen, including an impromptu trip to the hair salon. I hated the highlights. But they were quickly fading out and, in a surprising turn of events, I liked the faded look better than the original.

Who would've thought?

"It was really nice," Avery said, his voice coated with nostalgia.

We hadn't had sex that night. Some part of me wondered if he'd make a move, but I don't think either of us were ready for that level of intimacy to come back. Cuddling was enough. In a way, it was more.

"I'm glad," Dr. Forner said, a warm, genuine smile spreading just so slightly across his face. "You don't have to tell me details if you don't want to."

I felt myself blush. There was nothing to be embarrassed about; we hadn't done anything. And even if we had, we were married adults for Christ's sake. But, for some reason, I felt uniquely vulnerable. As if the entire world could see through that large window in Dr. Forner's office, through my jeans and long sleeve t-shirt – straight to a very naked *me*. I felt entirely exposed. Dr. Forner seemed to catch on to the general discomfort in the room and very abruptly changed the subject.

"Let's go back a bit. I remember you both mentioning a few times that since Gracie died, you haven't really had much of a partnership. But I find it hard to believe there weren't good times that happened over the years, even if they were just sprinkled throughout."

I looked at Avery. He looked at me. I'd told Dr. Forner in the last session that good times had happened. That there had been little things here and there that were positives for the both of us. I guess he just wanted us to go into more detail. Maybe this was his form of reverse psychology. Maybe he thought I'd stand up and yell "We DID have good times, Dr. Forner! We've been in love this whole time!" But love-addled outbursts like that are fictitious at best, and I was never one for dramatic displays of romance.

Avery and I both looked ahead. It was odd that mentioning Gracie had become normal. My mind became a highlight reel in no particular order – a jumble of memories, replaying fights, nights spent alone in bed, tears in the nursery, packing up the nursery, engagement pictures, wedding pictures, maternity pictures *so many pictures – where had I put all the pictures?* – date nights, unanswered phone calls, handwritten love letters, long talks in the car. So many memories. And, to my surprise, no small number were happy ones. Even times after Gracie died. It's so strange how we classify time – generalize everything. There *had* been good days. There *had* been laughter and joy and smiles and good sex and great food, and sometimes great sex and good food.

There had been cuddles on the couch, movie marathons, pumpkin patches, and dinners out. How had I blocked all of those out? Where had those memories gone?

I remembered one night in particular, a few nights before our wedding. In the days and weeks leading up to it, so much of my thoughts revolved around what role my mother would have played had she been there. Picking out the dress and the flowers and the invitations – so many things moms are supposed to do. So many things she couldn't. I remember laying down on the bedroom floor, last minute seating chart revisions strewn around me, my head resting in his lap as he stroked my hair slowly and listened to me cry. I didn't feel like a burden. He didn't rush me or make me feel weak. He didn't judge me for showing grief at a time that was supposed to be happy. He just sat there with me, holding space for me as I grieved. That was the Avery I had fallen in love with.

"There have been good things," I said softly, more to myself than either Dr. Forner or Avery.

Those things happened. But it was like my mother used to say – they were served on a trash pail lid. What she meant was that even the best things aren't that good when they're presented alongside bad ones. There had been so many good things. But there had been, objectively, more bad ones.

Like when we got into a fight at one of those dinners out, and Avery told me he treated me better than I deserved.

"Try finding someone who puts up with your shit. You can't. I'm the only one who'll deal with you. You're fucking crazy, Odette. For real. Fucking insane," he'd told me, loudly as a waiter passed by to deliver waters to the table behind us. The waiter looked at me and smiled sympathetically, and I'd wished so badly in that moment to disappear. Avery apologized later, after leaving me at the restaurant for half an hour and then circling back to get me. But the words he said didn't disappear. They clung to me just like every other bad memory.

"I want you guys to do a little exercise," Dr. Forner said, taking out two legal pads from his desk drawer and two pens from the little black metal holder on top of it. "Write each other a letter describing one good memory you have and what it meant to you."

He handed us the writing materials and reached for his phone in his pocket.

"I'm going to set a timer. I don't want to rush you, but I'd like to devote the next half hour to this so we can process it next time. So once you both finish, you can take the letters with you and we'll swap them next time and discuss. Sound good?"

"Sounds good," I said.

Avery nodded.

I held the pen in my hand and set it to the stunningly white paper, my fingers bracing for the memories to come flowing through them.

"Dear Avery," I began.

Dr. Forner interrupted my stream of thought by putting his pen in the air, giving us the universal symbol for "one more thing."

"Don't feel like you need to finish these today," he said. "If you need to, go ahead and work on them throughout the week and bring them back."

I nodded and Avery gave an awkward thumbs up that made me giggle, which in turn made him smile, which made me smile. It was a cute little moment that I, in a way, wanted to use as my one memory. But that was a cop out. I'd have to be more original than that.

I looked down at the pad and pen, the two opening words begging for the company of others.

One good memory. One good memory. One good memory.

CHAPTER

NINE

———

"WHAT HAPPENS AT THE STATION…*stays* at the station," Daws announced, shoveling an unhealthy helping of mac and cheese into his mouth. It was a shift favorite – that and fried chicken. For a shift of 9 men, none of whom had any culinary skills beyond opening a box, picking up a giant container of fried chicken and pasting together some mac was easy enough. I cooked on nights I was on the engine or the back ambulance, but those were occasional, and the rest of the time, we settled into less than stellar nutritional habits. Taylor, for being so lanky, could put away easily twice as much as anyone else on the shift, and go back for thirds and fourths a couple hours later like it was nothing. Rommie, still new to the shift and the way meals played out with us, still looked horrified as each fireman heaved an ungodly amount of processed food on his plate.

"I don't know how you guys do that," he said, sifting through the salad he'd made for himself. He'd also grabbed a piece of fried chicken and a spoonful of mac. But the salad was the majority of his meal. I was impressed by his will power – not for resisting the urge to cover his plate in fried food, but for his ability to do it while under the most extreme peer pressure to do the opposite.

"Rommie over there eating like a fucking rabbit," Captain Howe said, his mouth solidly full.

"Gotta keep in shape, Cap," Rommie replied.

"Round *is* a shape, you asshole," Deli chimed in, faking a terribly inauthentic Italian accent and patting his stomach, of which there was very little to showcase. Everyone had a *thing*, and his was using a different accent every shift. He was remarkably good at staying in character -- usually maintaining it through every call during the course of the day, and breaking only if the Chief stopped by -- and remarkably bad at the accents themselves. But he was as dedicated to his art as he was to his body. He worked out religiously, managing to eke out a couple hours a shift, every shift.

I laughed and leaned back. I didn't ever eat much at the station. I snacked a lot and took smaller portions for meals just so I wouldn't make a poor choice. Once, early on in my career, I'd indulged in a bit too much lasagna and garlic bread – taking seconds of the insanely rich, cheesy goodness – just to get a box right after I put the last forkful in my mouth. I felt fine until I jumped off the rig and turned quickly to pull the line off. The entirety of the meal, which hadn't quite had time to settle in my stomach yet, came pouring out of my mouth and settled on the grass next to the engine. I was mortified.

"Never eat more than your mask can hold, rookie," a senior guy said, laughing. He pushed me aside and pulled the line. Thankfully, the box wasn't a showstopper. But the lesson stuck: Never eat more than you can manage if you have to run, walk quickly, turn sharply, or do any real physical activity right after.

I looked over at Parker, who had finished his food and was sharing a quiet conversation with Stern. He caught me eyeing him and gave me a look, one that I couldn't quite define, and kept talking.

"Fucking Carrigan can eat more than you, Rommie!" Vick chimed in. He was adorably late to every joke, and this was no exception. I laughed. There was something endearing about all of them. Each with their own stupid quirks and habits.

"Give him time, Vick. Give him time," I said, patting Rommie on the back. "He'll learn."

The table was split, with about three different conversations going on at the same time, as usually happened, multiple people adding their voice to the inharmonious chorus here and there, before moving on to the next. No one stayed in a single conversation for more than a few moments.

I looked at my phone. I had been writing my letter to Avery in my notes, a little bit every day since the last session. I'd gotten remarkably little done sitting with Avery and Dr. Forner seemingly staring at me (I knew they weren't, but it still felt that way), and the next session was two days away. I needed to finish it. Working on it at the station was uncharacteristic for me – I tried my best to keep the station and home separate. And, oftentimes, it felt like the station was more *home* and home was more *work*. But the letter had to be finished. I read over what I had so far:

> *Dear Avery,*
> *I'm sitting here trying to think of a good memory of us and I know there are many to choose from. It's hard to pick one.*

The letter was so short I was able to easily transcribe it from the legal pad to the notes in my iPhone. It was pathetic. Almost a week and I hadn't been able to write any more than two sentences. It's not that the memories weren't there; it was that I felt like writing them down took them out of a vault and blasted them into the warzone that had become our marriage. Removing them from the safety of my mind meant exposing them to the harsh realities of the present – it meant taking them from a place of peace to one of stray bullets and misdirected bombs. I didn't want to lose them. I wanted to keep the good things safe, hold them close to me, inside me, where nothing in the cold, unforgiving climate of our current state could harm them. But I also knew that keeping them locked up was, in a way, allowing them to erode. They weren't able to breathe, to grow stronger with the sunlight of remembrance. They were degrading, slowly but surely. So I plied one out.

I remember that time we picked up Leo from the shelter. You were so excited. You picked him up and...

"Are you gonna go on that or is the ambo just gonna leave without a driver?"

I lifted my head to see Felix looking down at me, pointing at the ceiling to indicate the flashing blue light and distinct tones of an ambulance run. I was shocked I hadn't heard it.

"Shit, yeah. Fuck."

I grabbed my water bottle from the table and clicked my phone off as I slipped it into my pocket.

I continued writing and erasing in my head the entire way over, during the call -- a patient refusal after a minor car accident in a parking lot -- and all the way back.

~~You looked so cute holding him for the first time.~~
~~I could see how much you loved him.~~
~~You really seemed happy to finally have a puppy.~~

Everything I wrote seemed stupid and pointless. He was probably going to come up with some sweet, romantic story of something I'd done years before, and all I could think about was the day we got Leo. But maybe that was enough? Maybe it didn't have to be a perfect memory.

When we got back, the kitchen had already been cleaned up and most everyone had dispersed for the night, so I took the opportunity to try to finish the letter.

> *You picked him up and you just seemed so happy. And seeing you happy made me happy. I remember the look on your face like it was yesterday. It's stupid, maybe, but I fell in love with you even more that day.*

"What're you doing, doll?" Parker messaged me.

The text caught me off guard. For a moment, oddly enough, I felt *taken*, like I was married again, and that text struck me like an intrusion, rather than a playful greeting from a man I loved. It felt like he was trespassing on something, like he was taking the space I'd made for Avery in my mind and usurping it. And, briefly, I felt a little angry, and a lot guilty, that I'd allowed it. But then he came into the bunk room, where I was laying on my bed alone, and smiled at me, and wiggled my foot with his hand, and slid over to me quickly and kissed my forehead gently, and everything else fell away. And I remembered that feeling of wanting versus knowing. The painful, debilitating difference between the love you have and the love you want. And as Parker gently removed his lips from my forehead and squeezed my hand, walking back out the door and leaving me by myself again, I realized I couldn't finish that letter. Because the memories I had with Avery were just that -- *memories*. And the life I wanted wasn't stuck in the past, it was *here*, in the *present*. It was the feeling of closeness and desire and need and want and *love*. Love like I hadn't ever felt it before. And maybe I wasn't meant to be with Parker. Maybe Parker wouldn't choose me. But I had to choose something. And I didn't want to choose the love I had. I didn't want to settle into a life lived of memories, a love sustained by the past, rather than nurtured by the present. I didn't know if I was strong enough to choose myself, to choose what was dangerous over what was safe. I didn't know if I could be the one that to boldly set foot on a new piece of land and plant my flag in it. But I *wanted* to be that person. Sometimes you can try to be the strongest version of yourself and, if you stick to the feeling long enough, you can actually fool yourself into becoming it. And then, other times, more frequently, you end up slinking back into the comfort of the person you were before. One of them is the one you're meant to be; the other is the one you end up being. Most of us end up living half-lives, because to fully live means to fully risk. And not many people can leap without a net.

I stared at the letter on my phone until the screen timed out. As I lay there, I replayed a highlight reel in my head – the good, the bad, the mediocre, the asinine, the ridiculous. I clicked my phone back on and went down a voluntary rabbit hole, swiping through hundreds of pictures of me and Avery from the past 8 years. I smiled at some, winced at others, teared up at the rest.

I loved him. I still loved him. And losing him, losing the us we were supposed to be when we made those vows seven years earlier, felt like losing a limb. But it also felt like gaining wings.

I wanted to want him. So badly. But I also wanted to be happy. And, there, in the place I was in the time I was, as the person I was, there was no happiness to be had between us.

Music always saved me. It was the blood that gave me life when everything felt like it was falling apart. When Gracie died, music kept me alive. Very literally.

As I sat there, trying desperately not to cry, I remembered a song I loved. A John Mayer song with lyrics that always struck me. "Slow Dancing in a Burning Room," it's called. That's us, isn't it? Me and Avery.

We'd always been dancing while the world around us – the one we built -- burned. Sometimes we danced together; most of the time we danced alone, making the most of the songs we played for ourselves. But the room was burning. And one of us had to get out. And perhaps, jumping out of that burning room wouldn't just save me; it would save him too. Sometimes you need someone else to push you out of harm's way if you can't see the danger. Or, if you're too lost to see the danger. Maybe Avery needed me to jump just as much as I needed to.

Maybe one of us just needed to wake up to the flames.

◆ ◆ ◆

That night, Parker texted me. I'd thought he was in bed, but apparently I was wrong.

"Finish it yet?"

"Finish what?"

"Casablanca."

I smiled. "Still on the first 10 minutes."

"Come upstairs."

It was after midnight and everyone was fast asleep, so I tiptoed cautiously out of the bunk room, using my phone flashlight to navigate around the beds and duffel bags.

When I got to the office, he was sitting at the desk with a bowl of popcorn and two sodas. He had a chair pulled up next to him for me, and the opening scene of "Casablanca" frozen on the computer screen.

"Ready?" he asked.

"For real?"

"Absolutely. If you keep it up you'll never finish the movie. I'm doing this to save you the insanity of never knowing the ending."

"I know the ending. I just haven't seen the movie."

"Then how do you know the ending?"

"Because I've read about it and I've seen clips."

"Sit your ass down, Lucy," he said playfully, grabbing my belt and lightly pushing my back into the chair next to him.

I smiled and put my head on his shoulder.

He winked at me.

"Here's lookin' at you, kid," he said. And he pressed play.

CHAPTER

TEN

———

I CANCELLED THE THERAPY SESSION scheduled for that Friday. I told Avery I was sick and, in a way, I was. In reality, I couldn't face the idea of unveiling a blank paper where my letter was supposed to be. I replayed the scene in my mind over and over again how I expected it would play out:

Avery would read his magnum opus, an eloquent, inspirational, romantic letter detailing the times in our lives he felt the most in love with me, moments that made him singularly happy. I would sit and listen, half hearing his words, half hearing my own heart beat as I would struggle to come up with an excuse for not having anything to present.

"Now Odette," Dr. Forner would say, "Avery's written a lovely letter to you detailing a very impactful moment in your lives together. I'm sure yours is just as meaningful to you. Would you mind sharing it?"

And I would sit there, the weight of the room resting on my shoulders, and I'd blurt out loudly and unexpectedly, perhaps even to myself, "I don't want to be with you anymore!" and run out like a petulant child.

So, wanting to avoid all of that, I cancelled the session. Avery was loving and doting those two nights after he came home from work in between my last shift and my next one. And that made it even worse. He was kind and attentive, filling me with tea and chicken soup and trashy magazines to distract me from the cold he thought I had. They did help, really. And I was grateful, albeit ashamed. I knew I needed to be up front with him, sit him down and tell him the truth – that it was over between us, simply because it had to be. But I needed more time. A few more days to breathe and think about the choices I had in front of me – the life I was running toward and the one I was fleeing.

I was grateful for the next shift, to be at work and away from home. I also felt like I needed to have an important conversation with Parker. Because if, by some slim chance, he would choose me if I chose him, I had to know. I tried not to give myself false hope. He'd never even implied that he would leave his wife for me, so even considering that possibility was unrealistic at best, and delusional at worst. But I wanted to hold onto the idea of it, even if just for a short time.

It was that idea that flitted around in my mind, bouncing from corner to corner, when I saw Parker on Saturday.

"I think I need to leave my husband," I said, somewhat out of the blue. We were sitting in the office at the end of the shift, around 1900. We'd all just wrapped up dinner and were taking a breather from an unusually fast-paced day. There had been more calls than usual, which was a blessing, because it kept me away from Parker and away from my own thoughts. Until now. Parker was leaned back in his chair, patting his stomach from an overly indulgent, but not uncharacteristically hearty, meal of mozzarella stick sandwiches and tater tots. Firemen eat like children without

parental supervision. In reality, firemen do everything like children without parental supervision.

"Wow."

He looked surprised. And a little concerned.

"Are you okay?" he asked, reaching out his hand palm up so
mine could settle inside.

"Yeah. I mean, no. I don't know."

He moved away and slid back his chair, locking his hands
together and placing them behind his head, elbows out.

"Is this my fault? Is this because of –" he motioned between
the two of us.

"No," I lied. "It was a long time coming."

It was. But it also wasn't. It felt like everything went back to
that sinking ship. If our ship was sinking before, Parker was a
drill, poking holes in every little point to make the slow leak
happen a lot faster.

He looked at me sheepishly, his *I don't believe you* look that I
loved so much.

"Really," I said. "It would've happened either way."

I swallowed, first realizing how dry my mouth was.

"I have a question, Parker."

"Shoot."

"If I chose you…"

"Don't."

"If I did."

"If the timing were different; if I'd met you seven or eight years
ago; if the stars had aligned for us, then absolutely, Lucy. I would
absolutely choose you. In a heartbeat."

That answer was equal parts sweet and deflating. He *would*

choose me. But he *wasn't* choosing me.

"This is good though, right? We still have each other."

For how long though?

I wanted to question him, to ask what I was to him besides "the other woman." To ask if that's all I was ever meant to be to him. But I couldn't. Losing Avery was enough. I couldn't face another pain. I couldn't be that empty all at once. I needed something to hold onto.

"Yeah. Of course," I said.

I tried to tell myself that I would've left Avery regardless. That Parker was the impetus, not the action. But only part of me believed it.

"C'mere, Lucy."

He swiveled his chair over to mine and stood up, putting his hands on my shoulders from behind and leaning down to kiss me.

"I love you," I whispered, without thinking.

I'd never said that to Parker before. I'd texted him hearts, which he'd returned. He called me "love" frequently – alternating between "love," "doll," and "Lucy." But neither of us had ever said that full sentence before.

I instantly regretted it. He pulled away and took a blatant step back toward his chair before sitting down excessively carefully, as if the squeak of the wheels should themselves be kept secret.

"Wow."

"I'm sorry."

"Don't be sorry."

"You don't have to say anything."

"I can't."

"Why?"

"Because I'm married."

"So am I."

"Yeah but it's different."

"How?"

"You're leaving him."

"And you're not leaving her? You're so sure it won't happen?"

"I don't know."

"Do you love me?"

He stared at me, unblinking.

"It's not that easy."

"Do you love me?" I repeated, slightly more forcefully.

His eyes gently pooled, little tears that he quickly rubbed away with the back of his hand.

Choose me! I wanted to yell.

But I didn't. I didn't give him an ultimatum or tell him he had to make a choice, because I knew I wouldn't be who he chose. But I wasn't ready to give up whatever it was we had. I wanted to hold onto him a little longer, even if he would never really be mine to hold.

"I have to finish up these reports," he said, turning to his computer screen.

"I'll leave you to it."

I got up and left, no good night kiss or playful banter to end the evening.

But when I got back to my bunk, ready to pass out early, or so I hoped, I got a text. It was from Parker, and all it said was "Yes."

CHAPTER

ELEVEN

I TOLD AVERY I NEEDED TIME TO THINK and I took a week off to visit Bridgett. It was a last minute decision, really. And of all the people to run to, my sister was hardly at the top of my list. But she was as far removed from the fire department as I could get, and I needed that. Plus, the idea of seeing my nieces made my soul feel a little more full, and I needed that, too. To my surprise, I heard from Parker more than Avery. He hardly ever texted outside of work, but on shift days -- the days he was there that I would've been had I not taken off -- he messaged me religiously. He gave me little play by plays, telling me about the meals they were having, the daily shenanigans, the asinine interactions, and the raucous displays of immaturity characteristic of the fire department. His texts gave me life. They were little reminders that he was thinking about me – that there was someone out there who felt connected to me in some way. When I missed him, which was every moment, his texts reminded me why.

Seeing Bridgett was painful and liberating at the same time, just as I thought it would be. She was never a bastion of support, and this trip was no exception. I spent most of the time with the girls, trying to avoid one on one time with my sister at any cost. She let me take them on little trips that had us gone most of the day every day, and since they were on spring break, it was the perfect opportunity for some impromptu excursions. We went bowling the first day, got manicures the second, went to the movies the third, hit he mall on the fourth, and visited the local ice skating rink on the fifth. Every minute with them was beautiful, but also inherently loaded. Because the fun girl-time I had with them should've been time I had with Gracie. They would've been so close in age had she lived. I could almost imagine the three of them playing and arguing and making up, sharing stories and eventually giving each other advice on boys and complaining about how their crushes were inevitably too famous and too old for them. I imagined we'd have gone to visit a lot more if she were alive.

Josie and Jenna had such big personalities. They were divas and princesses, but they were also kind and generous and thoughtful and, in ways far beyond their years, empathetic. They didn't know a lot about Gracie except that she was their cousin in heaven. And most of the time, I assumed they'd forgotten. But sometimes, occasionally, they'd bring her up in a way that made me smile and break on the inside all at once. Like when we went to the mall and I got them matching neon rainbow skirts, the kind their mother wouldn't be caught dead buying, and Josie asked if we could get an extra one for Gracie so she could look at it from heaven and match her and her sister. I didn't believe in anything religious, but Bridgett did and she was the one who told them about Gracie, so that's the explanation they got. And I was OK with that. I never pictured her in heaven, per se, because I never subscribed to the idea of an afterlife. But I wanted to believe that somewhere, somehow, Gracie was home. And so I bought the extra skirt and gave it to Josie, and when we got back to her house, she set it in her little beanbag chair by her bed. She looked up to the ceiling and whispered, "That's for you, Gracie. Whenever you want to wear it." And I smiled and gave Josie a hug and tried desperately not to cry, because I think Gracie would have loved that skirt and her cousins and that day we had together.

Those moments are so complex, because they fill you with grief and gratitude all at once, and you wonder how your heart can have enough space to hold the magnitude and intensity of both emotions at the same time. But it just does. I don't think our hearts have limits. We feel endlessly and without confinement. Every day, every hour, every second.

On the last day, after a week of evading serious conversation with Bridgett, she cornered me.

"Let's go to lunch. Just you and me before you leave."

"What about Skylar and the girls?"

"I already talked to him. He'll watch them. Come on. One on one time with my sister! We never get that."

She was artificially excited and it showed. I could tell she was just itching for an opportunity to ply me for information. But I had no excuse and my flight didn't leave for another five hours. So we went to lunch.

It was her choice, a little hamburger place that was owned by the most adorable old married couple. Hank and Louise had been the proprietors of *The Hamburger Helper* for more than 40 years, and they swore the box brand stole the name from them (though the packaged dinner company predated the restaurant by more than a decade). They were sweet and kind, and acted like each person who came in, regulars and out-of-towners alike, was family. I'd only met them a few times, once in a while when I came up to see Bridgett and the girls, but they remembered me every time. It was heartwarming.

The menu didn't feature many options, and they hadn't modified it in about 15 years, but they didn't need to. The staples were perfect. I ordered a regular burger with fries and a coke, and Bridgett went for a milkshake and fries.

"I'm on a diet," she whispered when I gave her an odd look as she ordered.

When Louise left (the couple were the servers as well as the hosts and cooks, so every order took about half an hour, if not more, to fill), I laughed.

"What do you mean you're on a diet?"

"I'm trying to lose weight."

"You look fine."

"I know. I just want to lose a few pounds."

"So you're getting a milkshake and fries?"

"I skipped the burger."

"Bridge, I love you, and you can eat whatever you want, but you know skipping one burger won't do anything, right? And you chase kids around all day. You look amazing. You're too hard on yourself."

Bridgett rolled her eyes.

"All this because I didn't get a burger? Jesus. Get off my back."

"Ok, ok," I sighed, replacing the word "back" with "ass" in my head. I couldn't talk the way she did, dissecting every sentence for proper, appropriate language. I talked like a firefighter.

I turned to the stack of napkins and started picking them out one by one, stacking them neatly on the table in an attempt to occupy myself until the food arrived.

"What're you doing? Are you 5?"

"Maybe."

Every time I saw my sister I thought the same thing: She wouldn't last five minutes in the fire house. She was too regimented, neat, orderly. Everything had to be done *her way*. She despised any words more vulgar than "heck" or "crap" and insisted that everything be cleaned up as soon as a mess was made. She was prim and proper in almost every way. Case in point: When her milkshake and fries arrived, she dipped the fries in the shake with her fork just to make sure her hands wouldn't get dirty, cutting each fry in half first to ensure the perfect bite-sized portions. It was excessive, but profoundly *her*.

"How're things with Avery?" she asked a few minutes into our meal, right as I took a bite of my burger.

I pointed to my mouth to indicate I was chewing and that she'd have to wait a minute, and then intentionally chewed longer than I had to just to avoid answering the question.

"Fine," I said once I'd chewed for easily 45 seconds. The burger had become mush in my mouth, and hardly appetizing, but the extra few seconds felt necessary.

"How's his work?"

"The same."

"When do you think you guys will try for another baby?"

"I really don't want to talk about that, Bridge."

"It's just that I think you'd make a great mom one day."

"I *was* a mom."

She paused, and I could see her tear up.

"You still are, honey. You always will be."

She said it sincerely, tilting her head and looking at me lovingly, like she could sense the emptiness I carried inside me. Like she saw it, even if it was just for a second.

"It's just that I know how much love you have to give and I'd hate to see that…"

"Wasted?"

"No. I wasn't going to say that."

"Then what were you going to say?"

I was getting defensive and I knew it. I just had no desire to have that conversation with her. Bridgett meant well, but she was inherently maternal, and while that was sometimes endearing, it was at other times simply irritating. She'd been that way for years, since the day the faucet screamed to be turned off and she'd begged me with her eyes to not fall apart, because she was, and no one can properly handle two breakdowns at once, especially when one is their own. That day, when I was 10 and she was 20, with no father to speak of and no aunts or uncles, she became the sister-turned mom that was forced to raise me. In her defense, though, she never acted like I was a burden. She never once complained about having to skip dates or college parties to take care of me. If anything, she treated the responsibility like a prize she'd won. Like she was profoundly lucky to get to be my caregiver. But for all of her kindness and patience, she was also critical, overbearing, and nosey. She insisted on knowing everything going on in my life, and oftentimes dictating it. She had been completely opposed to my career in the fire department, even going so far as calling Avery to ask him to talk me out of it. And she never really liked Avery, either. She always said I could do better.

I looked at her and thought intently and loudly, as if I could will her to hear me.

I'm leaving Avery and, guess what! I'm probably never having another baby. So. Enjoy the information you wanted SO badly!

She seemed to read my mind and said "I just want you to be happy" before adding "you and Avery."

I'm happy with Parker.

"I know," I said, pushing what I wanted to say aside in favor of what I should say. "Don't worry."

We ate in silence for a few minutes before she changed the subject, telling me about Skylar and his twin brother and their weekly podcast where they talk about sobriety and god and the role of religion in recovery from substance abuse.

"It's nice that he's found that," I said. "I just can't really relate to it, y'know? God. What god? What god would fuck up the world so much?"

She looked at me, disappointed, like I'd just told her I'd become a stripper on the side and dealt meth out of the trunk of my car.

I knew I was starting something and, in truth, I hadn't really thought about what I was saying before I said it. But when the last words came out of my mouth, I knew I'd gone too far. At least for her. Religion wasn't up for debate with her, so we just never discussed it. Like many things. If you don't talk about it, it doesn't exist. Me and Avery subscribed to that idea, too.

Look where that's gotten us.

"I'm sorry," I said, pre-empting her inevitable rebuttal.

"Maybe let them choose what they believe in."

Her response was surprisingly calm and understanding, and I felt relieved, if not bewildered. I nodded and smiled, a little gesture that I hoped showed her that I could be reasonable, too.

"Finished?" she said abruptly.

I was three-quarters of the way through my burger and half-way through my fries, with every intention of finishing them, but I decided this out was better than no out so I said yes. I paid and we left, enduring the sweet silence that comes when two siblings have nothing to say to one another but they still, in some way, enjoy the company only that close a kinship can provide. I needed my sister. Maybe not her nagging or her incessant need to control me. I needed the knowledge of her – the fact of her. I needed to know that, no matter what, she existed in the world, ready to pick me up if I needed her, even though I never really did. And, I think, in a weird way, she felt the same.

When I left for the airport, she hugged me harder than she had in years, in a way that seemed to tell me she knew, without knowing, how much I was hurting. How badly I yearned for something I couldn't have. For the reason behind my necklace and the reason behind my heartache. She couldn't know about Avery or Parker or the feeling that comes from the enduring question of what could have been. But she knew the fact of it. She knew that the feeling existed. And that was enough.

"I'll see you soon, Odette."

"See ya, Bridge," I said, holding her even as she started to pull away.

I hugged Skylar briefly and picked up both girls one at a time, kissing their cheeks and tickling their sides as I walked out. I knew what was waiting for me when I got home. I knew the conversation I needed to have wouldn't be a pleasant one by any means. But I also knew it needed to happen. On the flight back,

I listened to my "Chill out" playlist, and ended up playing "Both Sides Now" by Joni Mitchell on repeat, at least five times. Eyes closed, I mouthed the words over and over, long since memorized, and felt myself sink into them like I was digging my feet into warm sand.

I inhaled every drop of reality the music sang to me, like the words were written for me, for that moment, for my story, and no one else. Like someone with a lens on my life had taken a pen and said, "I know this feeling," scribbling down words that came from a hidden place in my little world that only I had access to. Music can do that.

As I listened, wondering what else in the world can make you feel like that, can make you feel so completely understood, I fell asleep. And, for the first time in a very long time, when I floated between two homes, two lives, two worlds, I landed. But I didn't land in one of them. I landed between them, turning to each one and walking toward it before turning back to the other. I woke up before I decided which to enter.

CHAPTER
TWELVE

I SAT AT THE KITCHEN TABLE, IGNORING my phone vibrating repeatedly until I finally just turned it off. Avery was sitting across from me, fidgeting with a beer he'd opened but hadn't started yet. To my surprise, it was Avery who asked to talk. I figured he could probably sense my distance over the past couple of weeks. He probably knew what I wanted to tell him. Sometimes – sometimes – he was intuitive like that. It was technically my shift and I was supposed to be at work, but I had one more day of leave, and Parker was blowing up my phone.

"You need to come back." "I miss you." "What're you doing, hot stuff?" "Daws brought in donuts this morning. They're dry. Bring more." They came in every ten minutes or so. We often did that on shift, spamming each other with messages so our phones blew up until the other answered. He didn't know I couldn't answer, so the texts continued. After the first several, I put my phone on silent. This conversation was one I needed to pay attention to. Avery deserved that much. The seriousness of the moment deserved it.

"How are you doing?" Avery asked. He seemed to genuinely want to know, his eyes a mixture of pain and concern.

"I'm OK. Tired. It's been a long…"

"Few years?"

I laughed. "Yeah. Several years."

He took a sip and set the bottle back down, turning it back and forth nervously.

"Listen, Odette. This is really hard."

"I know."

But I didn't know. Not really.

"I know I'm the one who suggested therapy for the both of us, and I'm glad I did."

His face turned a little more red, and he took his hand off the bottle, instead using his fingers to fiddle with his wedding ring, twisting it forward and back, forward and back. I'd stopped wearing mine months before, and just then realized he still had his on.

"I just don't think we can make this work. It's too broken."

I just looked at him. I felt my mind clear of everything – every thought, every emotion, every reaction. I was completely blank. And then, as if someone had flipped a switch, I got really, really angry. Which, as a reaction, made absolutely no sense, because I'd been planning to tell him the same thing. But he beat me to it. There's something weird about being blindsided by your own decision.

"So you want a divorce?" I said.

I wasn't crying. Yet. If I was angry, I couldn't cry. I never cried when I was mad. So as long as I channeled everything through "the lens of aggression," as Dr. Forner called it, I'd be fine. I had it all figured out. I wanted to have it all figured out.

"I think so."

*You think so or you **know**.*

As if he could read my mind, he followed with, "To be honest, I'm not entirely sure yet. But I know this isn't working. We both know that."

He'd started crying, not audibly, but visibly – little tears bubbling and dropping, bubbling and dropping, two by two down his cheeks -- slowly and uniformly, as if they were dancing together, a little bit of heartbreak choreography.

I realized it was pointless to feel anything other than relief. I didn't have to do it. It was done already. He'd pulled the trigger. He'd started the bleed. I didn't have to. All I had to do was tend to my wounds and go.

"I know this is hard. I'm so sorry, Odette. You know, or I hope you know, for me, you're it. I won't find someone else. You're my someone."

"Then why do you want a divorce?" I asked, my voice cracking a bit at the end, which I was all too conscious of.

"Because love isn't enough."

Isn't that a song?

Sometimes Love Just Ain't Enough? That *is* a song. One I hadn't heard in years. But the chorus ran itself through in my head as I sat there, trying not to mouth the words in some sort of ironic display of disbelief.

It's funny how songs mean different things at different points in your life. I must have heard that song a million times but it didn't have any meaning until it struck me then. *Sometimes love isn't enough.*

"Are you OK?"

I had started crying more, and Avery handed me a napkin from the center of the table, a little gesture showing he was still on my side – we were on the same side, after all, weren't we?

"I love you, Avery," I said. And I don't think I'd ever meant it more. Not because we were ending things, but because we had *something to end*. And that meant we were giving up.

We sat in silence for a few minutes until he held out his arms. I moved over to him and sat in his lap, my arms around his neck, head resting on his shoulder. He held me so tight then. So tight I thought I might burst. But I didn't tell him to stop; I didn't want him to. I wanted to hold onto that moment for as long as I could. The dogs came over one at a time and sat with us, as if they could sense the sadness we felt. After what seemed like too little time and altogether too much, he let me go and I moved back to my chair reluctantly.

"You can take the dogs. I know how much they mean to you. I'll just forget to feed them anyways," he laughed.

He would never forget to feed them. He just wanted me to be happy.

"I'll move," I said. It took me all of 30 seconds to decide I didn't want to stay in the house filled with our memories together – some that made me smile, but many I wanted to forget.

"Are you sure?"

"I'm sure. I'll find someplace as soon as I can."

The practical side of me had kicked into full gear, ready to move forward with efficiency and expediency. A task had to be completed and I was going to take care of it. Compartmentalize. Do what you have to do first; feel later.

"Okay. I can help you look?"

"No that's fine. I got it."

Leo licked my hand and I patted his head gently.

"Do you want me to stay somewhere else until then?" I asked.

"No, no that's fine. I've been on the couch anyway. We'll just keep it as is."

I nodded and we both looked at each other. I reached across and stroked his cheek lightly. His beard was soft and prickly. He closed his eyes and bent his head, and I felt the defeat rise out of him and fill the space between us. The air was thick with it. Defeat and regret. Like two fighters duking it out for first prize. It had been a while since we'd had that kind of closeness – since the night of the movie – and it felt strange but normal at the same time. So odd it was to hurt over something I'd already so obviously lost. So odd to feel so much pain over something I was going to end myself had he not done it. But it wasn't who did the ending that hurt. It was the ending itself. It was the fact of it that stung.

♦ ♦ ♦

I picked up overtime the next day, just to get out of the house and, thankfully, the station where I was placed was busy. I only had a few moments here and there to think about the situation, none of which were spent looking for a house. I just couldn't do it. I knew I had to. I was resolved to the fact of it, but not the reality of it. I knew it was happening, but it felt like it wasn't happening *to me*. And there was a startling difference. Before we'd gone to bed the night before, Avery and I had decided that a month was a fair amount of time for me to find somewhere else to live. I pushed for shorter, but he insisted I take the time I needed. And I appreciated him for that. I appreciated him for a lot of things.

When I got home the day after my shift, Avery had already gone to work, but he'd left a note on the counter for me, along with a bouquet of red roses.

"Dear Odette,"

It was the letter we were supposed to write in therapy. He'd finished his.

"We're supposed to tell each other our happiest memory together. There are so many. I remember the time we road tripped to see your sister and I almost fell asleep driving so you took over and got us lost somewhere in the middle of nowhere, and we ended up pulling over to sleep. Only we didn't sleep – we spent the whole night eating gas station snacks and talking about our favorite movies and things we wanted to do together. I remember when we got Leo. I was so excited, but I could see how much you wanted him, and that made me even happier. I've always loved seeing you happy. I'm sorry I couldn't make you happier. That will always be my greatest regret. I remember when we were first together, you'd fall asleep on my chest and I'd feel so peaceful listening to you breathe (and snore) so sweetly. I miss that. I will always miss that.

I don't regret wanting to go to counseling, or going to counseling. I think, up until this letter, I was all in. I wanted to do anything to save this. But when I started writing, I realized how much we used to have, and how little we have of that left. And I realized that we're not holding onto the idea of the future; we're holding onto the past, and everything we used to be. I want you to know I don't regret a single thing. You have been the greatest joy of my life – I mean that."

He closed it with "And you do snore," with a misshapen wink

beside it, and I giggled through my tears. I held the letter close to my chest and crumbled into a ball on the kitchen floor. I cried like I never had before. It was like my entire body felt the loss, not just my heart. Like every part of me that Avery had touched, which *was* every part, came together to mourn him. I cried all night that night. I don't think I slept at all. When I got out of bed, I was deliriously tired, not from lack of sleep, but from the exhausting reality that had only hit me after reading Avery's letter. I found it insanely ironic that we'd had the same reaction to that assignment. We were still so alike, in so many ways. I got ready for my shift, quietly as always, so as not to wake Avery on the couch. Only this time, as I left for the station, I took an extra second to look at him, nestled under a too-small throw blanket, Leo asleep at his feet. That second wasn't long enough.

CHAPTER
THIRTEEN

———————

"I FOUND A PLACE," I TOLD DAWS, sitting across from him in the bunk room, each of us laying on our stomachs on our beds. It was a thing we did when no one was around – like two middle schoolers sharing secrets. He was the only one who knew about my problems with Avery (with the fact of Parker purposefully excluded from his knowledge of the situation) except for Parker, and I was trying my hardest to avoid Parker at all costs. It had been easy so far, since the last shift was his day off. Today would be harder. But he'd had a few long calls already, so one-on-one time wasn't exactly happening organically. It was already almost lunch time, and Daws and I were both on the back ambo, so we were taking a few minutes to ourselves before things inevitably picked up again. It had been six days since my talk with Avery, and on Day Four I'd finally brought myself to make an inquiry on a rental. And it had worked out perfectly – as perfectly as it could in that situation. "Oh yeah? Where?"

"This house on Cedar Street. It's a townhouse, but it's month to month, so it's perfect. The woman who's renting it out is really nice. She's letting me move in on Thursday."

"This Thursday?"

"Yeah. Four days."

"Damn."

"Yeah."

"You need help moving?"

"No. Avery said he'll help me. I'll be fine."

He gave me a look. He'd been divorced once, but his was less than amicable, so his experience with this sort of thing was far different, and he was ever skeptical of Avery's motives.

"Maybe I should help."

"No, really. I'm fine."

He nodded and held out his hand.

"Really? Now?"

"Secret handshake makes everything better."

Daws was, in every way, a 12-year-old in a 35-year-old's body. And I loved it. We hadn't been that close until a few months earlier, when he'd randomly opened up to me about his mom dying. We connected first based on that, sharing a similar sadness out of very different situations. His had been of early onset Alzheimer's. Mine had been from alcohol. Both were slow until they weren't. Both of our mothers had been stolen from us, just from different thieves. And, from that, we had the basis for a friendship. I told him almost everything, except Parker.

I hit the back of his hand with mine, then fist pumped three times, backslid his arm against my arm, followed by two claps and a sideways wave. He was right. It did make me feel better.

"Starting over isn't always bad, Carrigan."

"I know. I just don't want to."

"Nobody does. I didn't."

I felt my phone vibrate in my pocket and grabbed it.

"How's my girl today?"

It was Parker. I hated it, but the text made me smile. I had wanted to avoid him. I had wanted to put everything behind me – and he was part of the *everything*. But I also wanted desperately to keep him, to cling to the normalcy that was my relationship with Parker. And so, without much effort not to, I texted him back.

"Eh. Make it better?"

Parker was like alcohol. The more you drank, the better you felt. Until you didn't. And then you drank more, and you felt better again. He was always great in small doses, and so much better in large ones. Until he wasn't. And then I backed off, and came back to him even more desperate. It was a vicious cycle, a Ferris wheel I was all too happy to jump on.

"Come upstairs."

"I'll be right back," I said to Daws, not waiting for a reply as I hastily hopped off my bunk and started up the steps.

Parker was at the computer in the office when I came up. He smiled when he saw me and motioned to the left, meaning there was someone in the hallway and I should be mindful. I walked in casually.

"How's your day, looo-tenant."

He gave me his signature "I hate when you call me that" look. I loved it. I loved being playfully professional with him, simply because he adorably and predictably hated it.

"Ran two fire alarms. So. Not to brag, but I'm a pretty big deal."

I smiled.

"You *so* are."

"Still in the hallway?" he mouthed, motioning with his head for me to check. I walked through as if I had a genuine reason to.

"All clear."

He waved me over.

I wanted to not want him. I wanted to mourn Avery without leaning on Parker. But he was a distraction. I loved him purely, but needed him selfishly. He was my warm sweater in a brutal winter. Or, perhaps more accurately, he was my life raft in troubled waters. He kept me from sinking.

I came up behind him and put my arms around his neck, resting my head on his. He kissed my arm tenderly and looked up at me.

"You're beautiful, you know that?"

I smiled and kissed his forehead.

"Nah."

"You are."

"Whatever you say, Parker."

"Well I say so."

I heard shuffling and rushed to the other side of the desk, ruffling through papers to seem like I belonged there. Deli came peaking around the corner and walked in, announcing his presence by yelling "I already did!" toward the kitchen as he approached. What he already did was anybody's guess.

"Hey guys. Turns out we didn't buy rolls so it's just burgers for lunch. Just FYI."

I looked at Parker and he looked back at me.

"Burgers with no buns, huh?" I said. "Low carb day?"

"I mean, if you wanna run out and get some but the burgers are already just about done and you know Cap doesn't like waiting."

I laughed. Yes, he hated waiting.

"That's fine, Deli," Parker said. "I'm trying to cut back anyway."

"Is that why you ate – what was it? Five pancakes this morning?" I said exaggeratedly, scratching my head with the back end of the pen I'd been fidgeting with.

"Yes, as a matter of fact. Get all the carbs out of the way in the morning. Go low carb for lunch. Carb load for dinner. It's science, Carrigan."

"Well you two can do whatever you want but I'm just letting you know we have no buns," Deli said, raising his hands to indicate the bunless situation was, in fact, no fault of his.

"Thank you. We're better for that information," Parker said jokingly.

Deli smiled and shook his head as he walked out.

"So," Parker said quietly. "Tell me all about it tonight?"

"All about what?"

"You know what."

I did. But I didn't want to talk about it. Not with him. Not yet.

"Maybe," I said.

I sat down and continued fiddling with the pen, clicking it over and over again until Parker grabbed my hand.

"Lucy."

"Sorry."

He looked at me and smiled, his sad, sweet smile that I loved so much. The one that said he understood me, even when I didn't really understand myself.

"It'll be OK."

"Will it?"

"Of course," he said. "It always is."

Deli yelled "Lunch!" so loudly it startled both of us, and Parker jumped up.

"That's a fire house for ya. Come on. Let's go eat our bunless burgers."

I followed him into the kitchen, into the raucous mess of men, laughing and carrying on a litany of conversations at one time – the typical kitchen fire station setup. When it felt like my world was falling apart, they were my anchor. And, in that moment, I was eternally, unequivocally grateful to be a member of that family.

CHAPTER

FOURTEEN

———————

I DIDN'T HAVE NEARLY ANYTHING PACKED by that Thursday, but Avery helped me move what I did have. I left most of the furniture – the rental came furnished and I had no desire to stay attached to the items we'd bought together. Keeping them felt wrong, in a way. You don't go in search of change and keep your suitcases full of the past. You let that shit go and get on your way. But some things were harder to part with than others, like the couch I had picked out – the softest one we'd found in the furniture store with cushions that sunk super deep when you sat down, enveloping you like a cloud. I remembered how much Avery had loved it. "It's like it eats you ALIIIIVE!" he'd said, laughing. That couch really did swallow you up in the best way.

And the kitchen table. It had been my sister's, but I had no use for it so I left it with Avery, too. All I really associated it with now were talks about the future, or lack thereof, and the past; the meals we had and didn't have; the memories we never got to make with Gracie. I only really took my things and some pots and pans. I bought new dishes and towels and bathroom accessories. Somehow, it felt better to start over, in a way. And I kept the marriage certificate and the pictures of us. When I'd asked if

146

he wanted to keep them, he looked at me and asked if I wanted to, and we just looked at each other for seconds that felt like minutes, and then I put them in the box labeled "assorted" and that was that. We hadn't decided that, and yet we had. Everything unspoken is still said, just not as loudly. You learn that when a marriage falls apart. You learn that everything you don't say is just as powerful as everything you do; you just have to listen closer to hear it. And sometimes, you learn not to listen at all.

So they went with me.

The rental on Cedar Street was only about 20 minutes from our house – Avery's house – so moving wasn't terribly inconvenient. We started early, grabbing donuts at his insistence as fuel for the day. In his own way, I think he tried to make it as fun as possible. There's nothing traditionally enjoyable about moving out of the home you built with your spouse, but he brought a sense of levity to it that was very much needed. The funny thing about amicable divorce is that everyone thinks it's so much easier than one that has each partner foaming at the mouth. But that's not always true. Watching Avery give little personalities to each piece of furniture and yell "ouch" in high pitched voices on their behalf whenever we bumped into something just to get me to laugh – that didn't make things easier. It did, for a moment. It made me giggle and forget for a second. And then it made me question everything. Question why it didn't work between us if we could have so much fun and be so *civil.* Truthfully, I think we had more fun that day than we'd had in years prior. He was trying; I was trying. And so neither of us really had to.

All the boxes were in by about 3 p.m., and he stayed to help me clean and put things away. By 6, we were both exhausted and ready to sleep. Oddly enough, until he started gathering his keys and wallet and putting his shoes on, I hadn't considered the fact that he'd be leaving. In my head, I suppose, I just assumed he'd stay. That this was our home now, not mine. I'd imagined that moment several times over the last few days – when we would be done setting everything up and putting everything away (or most things) and he'd have to leave. But somehow, in the hectic, nonstop movement of the day, I'd forgotten about it, or maybe just pushed it away. But there it was in front of me – the startling, cold reality that this was my home, not Avery's. That he was leaving not for the night, but for good. That this wasn't a trip I was taking or he was taking, but a decision we'd made. I tried to stay composed, to make things just a bit easier for him. I knew if I cried he'd feel worse, and potentially feel obligated to stay. And as much as I wanted him to, if for no other reason than to not deal with this new life alone, I didn't want him to feel like he had to, or to second-guess what he knew he wanted. But as he leaned down and kissed Leo's floppy little ear, and told him he was a good boy and he had to take care of his mama now, I fell apart. I ran to the bathroom and shut the door, letting myself fall to the floor and crumple like paper onto the cool tile.

Avery burst in with little regard for the idea of privacy, but I didn't care. He gathered me into his arms and held me, his head resting on mine, soothing me with little "shhh's" and slowing his breathing to help regulate mine, which had become rapid and harried.

"It's gonna be okay. Everything's gonna be okay."

I wanted to believe him, but I didn't. It wasn't just the idea of the marriage being lost that hurt. It was the loss of normalcy, the feeling of uncertainty. The idea that everything in my life that I'd known as fact was crumbling around me, and I hadn't the slightest idea what to do.

I felt like I couldn't breathe, like the weight of each and every decision I'd made over the last seven years, specifically the last six months, was bearing down on me *hard*. Whenever we got a call for chest pain at the station, we always asked "What does it feel like? Is it like an elephant sitting on your chest?" If I'd have been asked that then, I would have said it felt like a semi was sitting on my chest. I couldn't breathe; I was trapped inside myself. The thoughts in my head spun over and over in circles that made me feel dizzy and overwhelmed and completely out of control. It stayed that way for more than an hour, and Avery held me for every second of it. Eventually, exhaustion took over and I fell asleep in his arms. I woke up as he gently carried me to the bed and covered me with blankets. I think he figured I was still sleeping when he kissed my forehead and knelt down beside the bed.

"Everything will be okay, Odette. I promise."

He softly stroked my cheek.

"I'm gonna go now. I'll call you tomorrow to check in."

I opened my eyes just as he walked out of the room. I heard him quietly say goodbye to the dogs before leaving the house. I wanted so badly to run after him, to beg him to stay with me just for the night. But that would've been selfish, and I knew that. I didn't want him for the reasons I should have, and he didn't want me either.

This is the right thing.
This is the right thing.
This is the right thing.

I repeated those five words to myself over and over and over again as I cried, eventually falling asleep to the little chant that became like a short nursery rhyme in my head.

I had a dream that night, another one that I was floating. Only this time, I floated back and forth between the new house and the old one, and every time I tried to touch down in one or the other, I floated right back up. I just hovered. I kept looking down, seeing everything from above. And the weirdest part was that I saw myself in each house. I saw myself with Avery in our old home and I looked happy. And I saw myself in my new one. I couldn't tell if I was happy there. I just felt ease, a sense of relief. A sense of calm. I wanted so badly to be those versions of myself. Either one. But I just floated above them, detached.

◆ ◆ ◆

The next day, I met Avery in the parking lot of the Dunkin Donuts near my rental. Moving out had been the difficult part. Getting divorced was easy. It was oddly official having him *serve* me divorce papers, especially since we weren't fighting or arguing at the time. We were civil. We were, in a way, cordial. Familiar. Married.

We hadn't really planned it out that way. It wasn't a scheduled thing of, Day 1: Move out; Day 2: Sign divorce papers. It was just how it worked out. We *had* decided not to do both on the same day. And then, that morning, he'd called and asked if I wanted to just get it over with. And, in truth, I did. I wanted so badly not to sign those papers. And at the same time, I wanted to walk away from this part of my life that had hurt so badly and step into something else. Something less painful. Something more sustaining. I felt so conflicted as I stepped out of my car and approached Avery's, the weight of memories settling on my chest. So many hours in that car. So many arguments and kisses and smiles and day trips. So much history can happen in a bubble. He had been my bubble. We'd been each other's, really. Filled with toxic air we just couldn't break away from, until now. He smiled as I opened the passenger side door, clearing off a couple of old receipts from the seat so I could sit down. We sat there for what felt like forever, neither saying a word. I looked straight ahead, staring at the row of trees across the way, pretending I could count their leaves.

I felt Avery take my hand in his. The envelope was on the console between us, untouched. Neither of us was ready. His hands were rough and calloused as they'd always been -- comforting in their familiarity. His eyes, dark but inviting, began to swell with tears. I couldn't not cry when he cried. No matter what, his heart had always been connected to mine. I felt what he felt. He reached across the center console and took me in his arms. I wrapped myself around him and felt an unburdening of months of pain in a single moment. My tears rolled down his jacket and slowly stained the cup holder between us, tiny droplets forming a portrait of everything we'd kept subdued for so long. We stayed like that, wrapped in each other's arms, breathing in unison, for minutes so slow and pregnant with feeling I couldn't begin to count them.

He pulled away carefully and wiped his eyes with his sleeve.

"I'm sorry, Odette. I'm really sorry."

"I'm sorry, too."

I thought I felt regret in his voice, but maybe it was just my own.

I signed the papers carefully, as if I would be tested on my signature. For some reason, autographing those forms felt like something that required the utmost concern. I wanted it to be right. Everything about this was fucked. At least the signature could be neat.

I placed them back in the envelope carefully and neatly, and set it back down on the console. I closed my eyes and covered them with my hands, taking deep breath after deep breath to steady myself. He pulled me into him and held me once again, squeezing me even tighter this time, as if he could force an imprint of me on himself. It felt so final and yet, a weird part of me felt like it was just a little hiatus. A brief interlude. This period would end and here we would be again. One day.

CHAPTER

FIFTEEN

—————

"**I** MOVED OUT," I announced.

Parker and I were sitting in the office, his feet propped up on the desk as he played with a deck of cards in his hands, shuffling and re-shuffling over and over again.

"When?"

"Two weeks ago."

I'd neglected to tell him not out of forgetfulness, but simply out of lack of desire to talk about it. The last two weeks had been spent crying, organizing, re-organizing, unpacking, repacking to donate, unpacking again, and crying. And more crying. I'd been quiet at the station, and our talks had devolved into hallway pleasantries. This was the first time in four shifts we'd actually hung out in our old space.

"Why didn't you tell me? I could've helped you."

I just looked at him. He wouldn't have. How would he have explained that one to his wife? *Be right back, honey. Just going to go help my mistress move out of her ex-husband's house.*

"I would have *wanted* to help."

"I know. I'm sorry. I just needed to do it on my own."

153

On my own meant with Avery. But Parker didn't need to know that.

"You're stronger than I am, Lucy."

"What do you mean?"

"You know when you're not happy and you choose to change your situation. That's ballsy."

"I mean, Avery chose it. I did what I had to given the circumstances."

"Still."

"I would've left. I was going to tell him that. He beat me to it."

"See? You're strong. I couldn't do that."

"You could. You can."

He took his feet down and put the cards on the desk.

"I made a promise. I can't break that."

"So did I. But it wasn't right. Sometimes you make the wrong choice; that doesn't mean you're doomed to stick to it for the rest of your life."

"Maybe."

"Parker."

He stared straight ahead.

"Someone should write a book about this," he said, laughing. Though I got the feeling maybe he was a bit serious.

"Maybe they already have."

We both looked at each other, and he smiled.

"Parker," I said.

"Yes?"

"Are you happy?"

"Right now?"

"Yes."

"With you?"

*You're not **with** me.*

"No. In general, are you happy?"

He leaned back and rubbed his forehead with his thumb.

"I'm content."

"But are you happy?"

"I don't –"

He was instantly cut off by the alarm sounding throughout the station. It was mine, an ambulance call that was probably hardly urgent. But I had to take it.

"Think about it," I said, as I walked out.

It ended up being a working code, and we were out for an hour. By the time we got back, everyone was in their bunks for the night, presumably asleep. Except one.

"Let's talk about this somewhere else. Somewhere not here," Parker texted.

"OK. When and where?"

"Tomorrow after shift. Parking lot outside Dunkin Donuts. I'll buy the donuts. You bring yourself."

"Always do."

◆ ◆ ◆

We left at the same time in the morning and I followed him over to the Dunkin Donuts, the same one I'd met Avery. He went in briefly and came back out with two coffees and a box containing six pastries: two apple fritters, two chocolate frosted, and two chocolate cake donuts. He never underestimated my ability to eat copious amounts of dessert, especially under extreme stress. The donuts were a necessity.

He came over to my car and I opened the passenger side door from the inside so he could get in. He handed me the coffee and donuts and sat down.

"Sweet," I said, opening the box.

"They had a special. Couldn't pass it up."

I put the box on the dash, but not before grabbing a fritter and putting it on a napkin on my lap.

He did the same, taking one of the cake donuts and managing to get crumbs all over the floor before even taking a bite.

"So what did you want to talk about," I asked. I knew, of course. How could I not? But acting coy was a habit of mine, especially in uncomfortable situations.

"What we talked about yesterday. Or started talking about."

He opened his coffee and put the lid on his lap, dipping the donut in and out carefully. I wondered how he could focus on something so trivial at a time like this, especially while I was shoving my donut in my mouth simply from sheer stress. There was nothing delicate about me in that moment, yet everything about him exuded poise and calm. Except the crumbs.

"OK. Go ahead."

"I don't know what to do."

"About?"

"You know what about, Lucy."

"You never answered my question."

"What question was that?"

"Are you happy?"

"I'm content."

"Yes, you said that. But are you *happy*?"

"It doesn't matter. I made my choice."

"That wasn't a death sentence, Parker."

"In a way, it was. That's what vows are."

"Well that's morbid."

"It's true though, isn't it? When you get married you promise to be with someone until you die."

"Yeah. And I'm getting divorced. Sometimes those vows don't quite work out."

He finished his donut and popped the lid back on his coffee.

"So you're okay cheating on your wife forever?" I asked, a bit more directly than I'd intended.

"I never said it was forever."

He grabbed my hand immediately after the words left his mouth, as if holding some part of me would soften the blow.

"I didn't mean it like that," he said.

I turned and looked out the window. Of course he did. How could this last forever? Or for any amount of time really?

How did I get here?

"Listen," he said, nudging my chin slightly so I would look at him. "I just need time to think, OK? Will you give me that? Just a little time?"

"OK."

"Can we talk about something else? Something less heavy?"

"Sure," I said, preparing to start an inane conversation about the donuts, just something stupid enough to take the swelling, rising stench of the shit of life out of the air for a moment. But his phone rang.

"Hey, what's up…no, got held a couple extra hours…yeah I'll be home soon…OK, just text me with what you need and I'll go to the store on the way back…you too."

He hung up and looked at me, as if apologizing with his eyes.

"Your wife?"

"Yeah. I gotta go."

He leaned in to kiss me but I turned away.

"Don't be like that."

"Parker. How can I not be like that?"

"Please."

He stroked my cheek with his thumb and probed my eyes with his.

"Please."

I nodded and he kissed me slowly, intensely, passionately. And I returned it. I kissed him with the intensity of love that is both beautiful and damned. Like that book I read in high school. I loved that book.

"Things are sweeter when they're lost. I know--because once I wanted something and got it. It was the only thing I ever wanted badly, Dot, and when I got it it turned to dust in my hand."

My favorite quote from that F. Scott Fitzgerald book came back to me then. And wasn't it so true? How everything you want the most seems to disappear in front of your eyes when you finally have it. Isn't that the irony of wanting? To truly get what you want is, in fact, to never get it at all.

"See you next shift?" he asked as he got out of the car.

"Absolutely."

"Keep the donuts."

"I was planning on it."

He smiled and closed the door, blowing me a kiss as he walked back to his car.

CHAPTER
SIXTEEN

D AWS SETTLED IN NEXT TO ME and handed me a cookie. "Deli's mom made them," he said with his mouth full. "And they're fucking amazing."

"Like crack," Stern yelled from the front of the room.

We were all gathered for the monthly training session with Capt. Howe, during which he insisted we watch YouTube videos of other, busier stations tackling other, more exciting fires. Truthfully, the videos were entertaining. They usually started out helpful, but after the first few real training videos, the captain inevitably left and, eventually, the videos deteriorated into "Jackass" clips and old footage we'd found of Taylor auditioning for a talent competition in high school. Deli had come across them months prior and they'd become a training day staple ever since.

In truth, the cookies were amazing. And the training day itself was never bad. But Howe was the kind of officer who would rather watch the videos and comment on them than actually go out and pull lines or practice attack strategies. So the videos were a little pointless, especially since they were the same ones over and over. Parker always had us do hands-on training, and he always trained with us. Just one reason I preferred him. Just one reason.

I was about to put the last bite of the cookie Daws had given me in my mouth when we got a call. I was on the front ambulance with Rommie, and he still ran to every call, regardless of what it was. His enthusiasm was endearing, albeit misplaced. This time, though, the urgency was appropriate. I was driving; Rommie was aide. He read the notes as we rode over. 17-year-old male. Self-inflicted gunshot wound to the chest. Unresponsive.

"Why would anyone shoot themself in the chest? If you're gonna do it, go for the head." Rommie asked.

"He's a kid," I said, jogging down the stairs. "Maybe he doesn't know any better."

There's something about this job that makes you forget you're a human sometimes. Those days hurt. You'd come up on somebody who actually, really needed help, and it was like your sense of belonging to a greater community – your sense of attachment to other humans – just came flooding back. You have to restrain it to do this. You have to forget that you're a person sometimes. Because people feel too much. And you can't feel for every single person. There's not enough of you to go around. But some calls can't *not* be felt. And this was one of them.

We arrived to find his mother, or who we presumed to be his mother, kneeling over him. He was laying in a sizable puddle of blood, and it looked like he'd been there a while. Too long for him to be viable. But you can't not try, not when there's a parent there. Not when they're screaming for you to save their son. Not when they're cradling his head in their arms and praying for god to do one good thing and give him a chance, when you know that chance is already long gone. You try anyway, because you can't not try. So we worked him for half an hour, more for her than any realistic purpose. There was no saving him. I knew that; Rommie knew that; the medic knew that. The engine company that arrived for additional aid knew that.

But you can't not try. Not when it matters to somebody like that.

Some of them hit you. Some calls make you look in the mirror and see too many memories, too many deaths, too many losses, too many people you couldn't save. This was one of those calls.

Rommie and I didn't say anything to each other on the drive back. I was struggling with it, not because of the death, but because of the mother. The way she sounded when she screamed for him; the way she cried as she held him. You don't forget those things. You see them when you close your eyes at night, and when you go on the next cardiac arrest because you want desperately for that to never happen again, knowing full well it will. But as shaken up as I was, I knew Rommie would be worse. That was his first trauma death; his first tough call. We all have a first. When we got back, I told Deli to keep an eye on him. Deli was his mentor, and a good one at that. I was confident he was in good hands. And when that was done, I went to the bathroom, cried softly into a paper towel, dabbed my cheeks dry and rinsed off my face. I said "okay" through a sigh into the mirror and straightened my uniform a bit, eager to regain the sense of purpose that came from wearing it. And then I left and forced it into the back of my mind. Because there will always be another call.

"Tough one?" Parker asked as I walked out. I nodded and he ushered me into the office. This time, the office wasn't a rendez-vous spot; it was a little respite from the cacophony of voices that was the station. I needed a little time to breathe, and the office was the best place to get it at that moment.

"Rommie OK?" I asked.

"Yeah. Deli's got him. He'll be fine."

"That was rough."

"Sounded like it."

"Take my mind off it?"

"Always."

He signaled for me to move from my chair to the one across from his at the desk. He sat down and got on his computer, pulling up YouTube videos of animals and fails and stupid people, little things that make your brain hurt, but in a good way.

"Can we hang out tomorrow night?"

I was surprised at my own question, given I almost certainly knew the answer.

"What time?"

"2100?"

"That's late."

"I know. Nevermind."

He looked at me, studying my probably obvious frown.

"No. Let's do it. Dunkin again?"

"You could come to my place."

He didn't say no but his eyes did, so we wordlessly settled on Dunkin. It struck me as odd that he'd come to the place I had with Avery but not the one I had on my own. It was almost like he preferred little meet ups in parking lots, like there was something dirty about them he was attracted to. They were the opposite of what his life was in every other way. He was the dutiful, responsible lieutenant at the station and the loving husband at home. With me, he could be adventurous and a little bit dirty. I think he liked that.

◆ ◆ ◆

The next night, he pulled into the Dunkin Donuts parking lot at precisely 2100. He had a bouquet of roses and a stuffed teddy bear.

"What's the occasion?" I asked when he handed them to me.

"You."

He was always too sweet. Almost unbelievably so. As if he had a repository of perfect phrases to say that he just kept dipping into over and over again, and it never ran out.

This time, I got into his car. He kissed me immediately – quickly and excitedly, as if he'd been waiting for that kiss for weeks.

"You look beautiful," he said.

I laughed.

"This old thing?" I said, jokingly.

I had actually put a nice amount of effort into my appearance. I was wearing black jeans and a bralette with a loose flannel over top. I wanted to show a little skin, and I thought he'd appreciate the look. He was wearing the soft blue t-shirt I loved – the one that felt like it was made of silk – and dark blue jeans. He hadn't shaved since the morning of our shift, and he had the slightest hint of a beard coming in. In every way, he looked perfect.

He turned on his phone and started playing a song. He signaled for me to join him outside.

"Dance with me."

The lyrics started right as he took my hand and pulled me close.

> *"Something in your eyes*
> *Makes me wanna lose myself*
> *Makes me wanna lose myself*
> *In your arms*
> *There's something in your voice*
> *Makes my heart beat fast*
> *Hope this feeling lasts*
> *The rest of my life…"*

"You hate this song," I said, looking up at him.

"Yeah. But you love it."

I smiled and rested my head on his chest, my arms folded around his neck. He **did** feel like home. We swayed gently under the stars, the weather just cool enough and warm enough to be inviting. It was the most perfect stolen moment I'd ever had. And in my happiness, I was acutely aware that the joy I felt wasn't mine. It was borrowed – taken – from someone else. But when he held me like that and kissed me gently, tenderly, sweetly, I felt like it didn't matter. Because in that flash of time, he might as well have been mine.

As we danced together, the song coming to an end, I thought about the empty house I would be going back to that night. I thought about Avery. He never would've done anything like this. He never would've even thought of it.

Then why do I feel like I miss him?

I forced my thoughts back to Parker. I had a soul-sinking feeling that tugged at my chest from the inside telling me this perfection wasn't meant to last, that I should enjoy it now while I had it.

While it was, even though it wasn't, mine.

CHAPTER
SEVENTEEN

F RIDAY ROLLED AROUND QUICKLY, and Daws organized a
shift trip to a local bar. If anyone was going to get the band
together for anything outside of the station it would be Daws. I
really had no desire to go. I hadn't talked to Avery in weeks (we'd
agreed not to talk for a while after I moved out and, honestly,
the lack of communication didn't feel much different than when
we were living together, which was, itself, disconcerting); I was
exhausted from too much overtime; and I desperately needed
some time alone. But Daws said it wasn't optional. So I put on
a tight black t-shirt and my best fitting jeans, and I even threw
on some somewhat-high heels for the occasion. And a little bit
darker eye shadow than usual, of course.

Howe wasn't invited, given there was no question that he
wouldn't attend. Parker said no. And Rommie was 19 and too
much of a rule-follower to try to get in underage. So it ended up
being me, Daws, Deli, Taylor, Stern, Vick, and Felix. Four of us,
including myself, piled into Taylor's car. And the other three went
with Daws. When we got there, it was packed, and I instantly
regretted my decision to go. There was also a huge sign that read
"Karoake Night: 80s" at the door, which made me want to leave

even more. I hated karaoke. Not for the singing, but for the loudness. So maybe for the singing.

"Fuck yeah! 80s night!" Felix yelled, jumping and hitting the top of the door frame with his hand as he walked through.

"Are you drunk already?" I asked. It was a half-genuine question. He rode with Daws so, for all I knew, they could've been pregaming the entire way over.

"Maybe a leeeeeetle bit," he said, scrunching his first finger and thumb together to make a "this much" motion.

"Oh Jesus," I said.

"Oh lighten up, Carrigan," Daws said. "Go get a drink."

I laughed and took him up on his suggestion, pushing my way past the distressing number of huddled bodies and eventually landing at the bar.

"Rum and coke, please."

"What's that?"

"Rum and coke!" I said louder, praying the bartender would hear that time and I wouldn't have to scream again. Being loud was something I detested, which was ironic given my profession, and the fact that I was surrounded by rowdy, noisy firemen for 24 hours at a time.

"You got it."

I chided myself a bit for not going for something a bit stronger. But I figured I had all night to work up to it. Just as I got my drink. Felix took the stage.

I watched him dance, or rather move frantically from one side of the stage to the next, as he attempted to sing "We Belong" by Pat Benatar. I sang along silently, mouthing words I didn't know and swaying my raised arm back and forth in support.

"Many times I tried to blah la la…Many times I la la la…" he mumbled several lines incoherently before reaching the chorus, which he knew perfectly.

I laughed, watching him hit his stride and catch the approval of many drunk onlookers.

"This guy's awesome!"

I looked over and saw an attractive, well-dressed 30-something man beside me. He was clean-shaven, with a short, slick haircut that boasted a substantial salary. He was wearing jeans that fit nicely without being too tight, and a plain black t-shirt that showcased biceps formed from far too many hours in the gym.

"What?" I yelled.

"This guy. He's good! You know him?"

"Yeah I work with him. And he's not good!" I said, laughing.

"Let's go somewhere quieter!"

I nodded. I had no desire to spend time with this unknown person, but the noise was a bit overwhelming. In this particular bar, there was a little event space in the back, where the quiet ones usually went. Typically, bridal showers rented the space out. But when it wasn't used, it was the prime spot for some gentle escape. Sometimes it was corrupted by random hookups, but we got lucky that night. Three people were engaged in a quiet conversation and that was it. The rest of the space was ours.

"So tell me about yourself, lady with the karaoke friend."

I laughed. "My name's Odette."

"Like Swan Lake?"

"Precisely."

"Very cool," he said, extending his hand. "Jesse."

"Pleased to make your acquaintance, Jesse."

He smiled and shook my hand.

He spent a few minutes asking me about my job and, surprisingly, seemed genuinely interested. He was an accountant, he told me, though he hated his job and desperately wanted something more fulfilling. We shared small talk about the number of times we'd both been at that bar before, the weather and how it was pleasantly warm, the singers who'd graced the stage thus far, and each of our drinks of choice. He was fun to talk to and carried a conversation well, but beyond that, I had no interest. He, on the other hand, seemed to think the conversation was leading down a different path.

"So, I'm not really sure how this works. But I'd love to take you out sometime."

He asked it sheepishly, with a curious nervousness that made me smile on the inside. It was sweet.

"Thank you for your interest."

I said it so platonically and emotionlessly that it reminded me of an automated voicemail message. I might as well have asked about his car's extended warranty.

"Oooof," he said. "That's a rejection if I ever heard one."

"No, it's not like that."

"I don't see a ring. Are you married?"

"Separated."

"Seeing someone?"

"Sort of. No. Not really."

"Okay…so you're single then?"

"No."

"So you're separated. Not dating anyone but not single?"

"It's complicated."

He studied me for a moment, his eyes probing me. I watched him put little pieces in place in his mind.

His eyes brightened as if he'd had an epiphany.

"Guy's married isn't he?"

I just looked at him, puzzled as to how he came to that conclusion in so little time, and wondering if somehow I'm more transparent than I thought.

"So you're a beautiful, separated woman on a beautiful night in a not so beautiful bar," he laughed, "and you're not bringing somebody home because you're waiting on a married guy who's probably home fucking his wife right now?"

"Ouch."

"Is he leaving her for you?"

"He said he has to think about it."

"What's to think about?"

"It's a hard decision."

"You should never be a hard decision to make."

"It's complicated. It's not that easy."

"It's her or you. It is that easy."

"You don't understand the situation."

"Look, I have no skin in this game. I'm gonna go talk to that girl in the red because she's been looking at me all night."

He pointed to a young woman in a short, red dress who had walked into the little room with two of her friends. She was, in fact, eyeing him up as we spoke.

"But I'll say this: you're gorgeous. You can have anybody. Don't wait on a guy who isn't waiting for you."

I nodded and smiled flatly.

"It was great meeting you, Odette."

"You too."

He walked away and left me sitting there, absorbing the words of a complete stranger who somehow seemed to size up my situation in a manner of minutes. He was right. In a way. But he was also completely wrong. I was waiting for Parker because I wanted him. And I loved him. And when you love someone, you wait. And wait. And wait. And you wait until you can't anymore, even if they're not ready yet, until they are ready, because love isn't conditional, and it isn't dependent on occasion. I believed that wholly, fully, in my core, I was waiting for my person. For him to realize there was more to his life than what he'd settled for.

But that night in the bar, as I swished my drink around in my glass and stared at the ripples it made, it occurred to me that maybe I was waiting for something that was never going to happen at all. Maybe I was waiting for an impossibility.

CHAPTER
EIGHTEEN

———————

P ARKER AND I LEANED AGAINST the hood of his car, his arms wrapped around me from behind. It was a beautiful summer night, the kind where the stars are a little too bright and the air is a little too clear and the universe seems to whisper *Enjoy this*. We were in a little park and ride a few miles from my house, and it was empty except for two cars at the far end of the lot. Far enough away that they barely existed to us. Just over a week had passed since my conversation with the stranger in the bar and, since then, I hadn't been able to get it out of my head. I didn't ask how Parker was able to get away for these, albeit few and far between, evening rendezvous we had. I didn't ask because I didn't want to know. I didn't want to imagine his wife sitting at home wondering where he was, because I knew that's what I would be doing if I were wearing his matching wedding band. But I wasn't. I didn't have that connection to him. All I had to consider was how to make these fleeting moments with him last a little bit longer – as long as they possibly could.

I knew Jesse Something was right. I knew the whole speech about choosing yourself and knowing your worth and accepting the love you think you deserve. I'd read the self-help books

172

(the backs and covers, at least) and I'd heard the motivational speeches. But it's different when you're facing it in front of you. It's different when choosing what you deserve means rejecting the one thing you want the most. It's different when doing *the right thing* means giving up *the best thing*. It's just different.

And so, with every intention of telling Parker I was done, I turned around and kissed him softly and carefully, absorbing the taste of beer from the Bud light he'd had earlier in the evening, and felt the thought fade away like sugar melting in a skillet. He gently rubbed my cheek with his hand and looked in my eyes.

"Do you love me?" I asked him.

He'd never told me. Not in all those days and office visits and meet ups. He'd never once said the word. Not out loud.

"Lucy."

"Do you?"

"You know the answer to that."

"Say you love me."

He stared straight ahead, his face changing quickly from contentment to concern.

"Why can't you say it," I asked.

"Because I just can't."

"I don't understand."

"I can feel it, but I can't say it."

"So you do love me?"

"Lucy."

"If you can say you feel it, why can't you just say it?"

He let me go and took a few steps forward, staring straight up at the sky, before turning around and looking at me.

"It's always been you, Lucy. Always."

I didn't know what that meant. For one, we'd known each other five months, not *always*. And secondly, it wasn't just me. That was the whole problem.

"Then pick me."

I hadn't meant to say it. I'd put the idea of giving him an ultimatum out of my mind, at least for the night – or so I thought. And then his statement pushed through the barrier in my head and gave me a moment of courage, a brief second where I thought, if I asked just then, maybe he'd say yes. Maybe he'd choose me.

"What do you mean?"

"You have to make a choice."

"Why?"

"Why? We can't keep doing this, Parker. What's the end game here? I'm your secret forever? You carry on with me while you're married? Where does that leave me?"

"I mean, we don't have to figure that out now."

"Why? When? When is the right time?"

He came over to me and took my hands in his.

"Hey. Look at me."

I looked up. His eyes were so kind, so thoughtful, so full of *love*. That stupid word that I so desperately wanted to hear him say.

"I need more time."

"You can't have more time, Parker. It's been too long already. How can this feel right to you? This isn't right. I love this. I love you. But I can't keep doing this. And neither should you."

For now, I was strong. I was confident. I was stable. But I knew, if this went the way I thought it would, I wouldn't be any of those things later. Or the next day or the next. I would be lost.

Giving him up would break me. I knew that.

Choices are funny things because they're twofold. People act like making a choice is hard, but it's not. Settling on a course of action is easy. Carrying it out is what's difficult. I think I knew what I had with Parker wasn't meant to last. I think something inside me always knew that the most perfect things are the things with built-in expiration dates. Maybe a taste of the fantasy is enough. Maybe asking for more is selfish.

He looked down at his hands and, for the first time in far too long, I noticed the wedding ring he was wearing. A simple gold band that looked worn. The same one that probably matched his wife's. The wife waiting at home. Waiting at home for the man who was with me.

"The ring is a symbol of the unbroken bond between the two of you." That's what the priest had sad at my wedding. That's what another priest probably said at Parker's. And yet here he was. Breaking it. And here I was. Helping him.

"Two weeks. Give me two weeks to think."

I looked away and studied a car in the distance, its lights off. The occupant was probably asleep, taking a much-needed nap on some cross-country road trip.

Maybe his name's Alan. And he's a traveling salesman.

I laughed in my head. What a stupid backstory.

My thoughts came back to Parker and I shuffled my feet anxiously. What did he need two weeks for? What could he possibly determine in two weeks that he couldn't figure out now? But it was Parker and he needed two weeks. I felt my resolve crumble at his fingertips.

"Okay."

"Thank you."

"Hold me?" I said, folding into his arms.

"Absolutely."

If he needed more time, and I was giving it to him, I could at least *be with him* in the interim. I could at least hold on to the piece of him I still had, regardless of how quickly it was slipping away, and how surely all of this would end. I could lie to myself a little bit longer.

We stayed in the parking lot for hours, eventually moving into the car. We didn't talk much. We just listened to music, indie songs we both loved, my head resting on his lap in the back seat. He stroked my hair, gently moving his hands up and down, up and down, until they felt like a part of me. He was a part of me, though. Maybe he always had been. And maybe that's what he meant when he said it had always been me.

CHAPTER

NINETEEN

____

HE'D NEVER KISSED ME LIKE THAT BEFORE. Like he was using my air to fill his lungs. Like I was his oxygen. He swept my hair aside and kissed my neck as he carefully, softly ran his fingers down my shoulder, over my collarbone, over each breast, down my stomach, over my thighs – lingering just long enough to quicken my breath. He was usually tender in bed, but this time, it was like he was being especially deliberate with every move. I felt like I was savoring it as much as he was. By the time I felt him slowly push inside me, every part of my body was yearning for him. I wanted him to move faster, to take me like he had before, but at the same time, I welcomed the slowness, the tenderness. Our bodies were moving together so gracefully, so in tune with one another, that we were, in those moments, barely separate souls. I closed my eyes, feeling every sensation within me match every craving of his. In every way, I belonged to him. In every way, he held my heart in the palm of his hands.

I'd never felt that way with a man before, not even before with Parker. Being with him was always special. It was always intimate in ways I couldn't describe. But this time, this time was different. It was like, for a short time, when his body and mine were connected so beautifully, we were beyond time. We existed, as our whole relationship had been built, outside of the world around us. In that room, in those minutes that passed so slowly and so passionately and all too quickly all at once, we weren't living for tomorrow or for the next day or the next. We were living for the pleasure in each other's bodies, for the grace in each movement, for the love in every touch.

We lay there when it ended, still so close, barely separated by skin. Quiet and unmoving. And then he looked at me. And I knew it was time.

"You decided, didn't you?"

He didn't have to answer. He didn't even have to nod. When he'd asked to come over, I knew what it meant. He'd never been to my rental house, and this would be the first and last time. I wanted to say no. I thought maybe if I did, it would delay things. Maybe he would reconsider by the next time I saw him. But I couldn't say no to him. I never could. And when he carried me to the bedroom without saying a word, I knew why.

I hadn't seen him in two weeks. He was either exchanged off or stationed elsewhere covering someone else. We didn't talk or message, even though I'd wanted to. I typed and erased more messages in that week and a half than I ever had before. I had the strongest urge to advocate for myself, to text him a litany of reasons why I was the right person for him. If he was to decide my fate as well as his, I wanted to at least make a good case for myself.

"I can be the best person for you, and here's why:"

I'd text him ten reasons. Twenty reasons. Thirty reasons. As many as it took to sway the decision in my favor. But I couldn't do that. The part of me that wanted to was silenced, just enough, by the part of me that was resigned to the fact that his decision had probably already been made. That there was nothing I could do at that point to change it, no matter how badly I wanted to. So, as challenging and heart-wrenching as it was, I waited. I waited for him to come to me. And there he was. Him and the decision I didn't want him to make, and yet I so desperately needed to hear. Closure is still closure no matter which direction it comes from.

I played with the hair on his chest with my fingers. His skin was so soft. I closed my eyes and took a deep breath. Everything was so perfect. Too perfect not to end.

"Odette."

He changed positions, leaning his elbow on the pillow. He hadn't ever called me that. My heart reacted to the stark contradiction of hearing his voice say my real name. I sat up and pulled the sheet over my chest. Whatever he had to say required a level of vulnerability that made me already being naked seem like overkill. I wished I could cover my ears and eyes and mind and heart all at once, just to avoid that moment. But I couldn't. So I settled for my body which, oddly enough, was the least important part of me he'd taken over.

"Don't cry." He leaned over and kissed my cheek. I hadn't even noticed I'd started crying.

"I'm sorry." I looked away and he gently nudged my face back to meet his.

"*I'm* sorry, Lucy. You know how I feel about you. If we'd met at a different time. If I had known you five years ago, there'd be no contest. And there really isn't one now. You're everything. But I made my choice before we met. And I have to stick with that."

"Are you happy though?"

"It doesn't matter. I made a choice already.

"It *does* matter, Parker! It *does* matter. Because choices aren't permanent. You can change your mind. I did. I chose you."

"You're stronger than I am."

"I'm not stronger than you. I just know what I want. I know what we have."

He gently stroked my arm and reached over, kissing each part of it until he got to my hand. I closed my eyes.

"You'll find someone who treats you better than I ever could. Someone who will give you everything you need. That person is out there – I promise. Someone just like me – but better." He chuckled, settling into the awkward silence after a forced joke.

"I don't want someone like you, Parker. I want you."

I felt like a petulant child crying over not getting the toy I wanted for my birthday. I was embarrassed and angry, and embarrassed over being angry. How many times can a person say they want someone before it becomes a futile attempt at begging for something already decided?

"C'mere," he said, pulling me into him and holding me tight with both arms.

I tried not to, but I felt myself crying softly and steadily into his chest. I inched closer and closer, trying to get my body to memorize the feeling of his, knowing it would have just this memory for the rest of my life.

I knew not to try. I knew there was no point. For the past two weeks, I'd played a scene like this over and over in my mind, each time with a slightly different ending. But none of them ended with him choosing me. I always knew he wouldn't. And yet, no matter how prepared I thought I was, in that moment, I would've begged to get 20 percent of him – any percent of his love -- just to stay in his orbit a little longer. Second choice, third choice, any choice. Hell, I didn't even have to be on his list. I just wanted to be *someone* to him for a little longer.

"People aren't meant to stay in our lives, Lucy."

"What do you mean?"

"I mean nothing good can stay."

"That's not true."

But wasn't it? What had ever stayed perfect? What had ever really lasted?

"We could just stay like this," he said. "We don't have to make it serious or official. It can just be like this."

I so badly wanted to scream *yes!* with every bit of air inside of me and throw my arms around him with delight. But I didn't move and I didn't answer. Because if I opened my mouth I would've agreed. I would've sold every part of myself to pay for his love. My silence, I knew, told him what he needed to know. It told him what I couldn't say out loud – what I wasn't strong enough to say.

Everything unspoken is still said, right?

We stayed wrapped in each other for hours, far longer than we should have. He'd told me he needed to leave at 5 p.m. and, by the time 7 rolled around, we'd barely moved. We weren't speaking; we were just existing with one another. Soaking in the last memories. Part of me wanted to make love to him one more time. To feel what I knew I'd never feel again. But perfection can't be achieved twice, and the last time was more perfect than anything I could have imagined. That's what I wanted to end with. That's what I wanted to remember.

"Lucy," he said, kissing my forehead and lifting my face with his hand.

I nodded, anticipating his next words. We both got dressed quickly. I caught him looking at me as he clasped my bra and pulled the straps over my shoulders. And I wondered if, maybe, he was trying to memorize me the way I tried to hold onto him.

I followed him to the door and held his hand tight, squeezing it as if I would die if even a bit of air passed between our closed fingers. He stood in the doorway and turned to face me, keeping his hand locked in mine as he kissed me. In a way, I wanted to remember the way his hands felt more than the kiss. We didn't say it, but I knew this wasn't just the ending of us as whatever nebulous romantic entity we had become; it was the ending of us as everything else, too. There would be no more late night talks in the office, no more sharing music and donuts in the car after shift. This was it. For him to move forward, for me to move forward, we needed to leave *us* behind. Every bit of us.

We stood there together, long after the kiss had ended. I didn't want to let go. How do you give up something that feels so perfect? How can something feel so perfect and be so unattainable? That was just it, really. We had tried so hard to not be *something*, just so we could be *something*. We couldn't label it because it couldn't exist. And what doesn't exist can't be defined. We lived outside of everything in the best possible way, and in the most heartbreaking way, too. Because to the world, we never were. He was Parker and I was Odette. Never Parker and Odette. Never spoken in the same breath, never sharing space in the unforgiving world of black and white. We were everything gray in the world. And nothing gray can ever exist for very long. Everything requires some semblance of definition. Where there is definition there is understanding, and where there is understanding there is acceptance. You can't accept what you can't define. In being undefined, we were doomed from the start. We never stood a chance.

My heart ached as he slowly released my hand, letting it fall at my side. My chest heaved, and I felt a sort of panic begin to set in, like I was standing at the base of a cliff, being slowly nudged off by some force I couldn't see. I couldn't stop it. I could just feel it happening, a slow fall and a rapid drop. But when I closed the door and watched him walk down the driveway toward his car, not looking back once, what surprised me the most wasn't the pain of losing him or the sudden, terrifying feeling of being alone. It was the relief.

CHAPTER

TWENTY

———

THE WEEKS PASSED SLOWLY, AND EACH SHIFT seemed to drag
on endlessly. I still saw Parker every third day and, in front
of the shift, we bantered back and forth and participated in shared
jokes. But beyond that, there was nothing. The beginning of
August brought unrelenting heat, and long summer nights. His
wife posted pictures on Facebook, their hands clutched together,
sharing posed laughter, snapshots of their trip from earlier in the
year. Rhode Island. I wondered if he was really happy in those
photos. I wondered if she knew he wasn't.

There are different kinds of pain, and humans use no shortage
of cliches to describe them. I never thought any of them were
very accurate. Being punched in the face or stabbed in the back
are useful analogies, but rarely correct contextually. Our feelings
don't translate well to physical comparisons. At least not normally. But seeing Parker and his wife together, however rarely it
happened, always felt the same. And as trite and overused as the
expression may be, it truly felt like having a knife thrust into my
chest every single time. As I looked at those pictures, plastered
all over Facebook just a couple of weeks after we'd parted ways,
I paused to accept the knowledge that they were taken while we

were together. Whatever together meant. She was his home; I was his escape. I don't think it hit me until that moment. That I was never his, and he was never mine. She was permanent; I was temporary.

Over time, I thought about *us* less. But never not at all. There were days I was able to distract myself enough that I could smile, and some days I even laughed. But always, living in discreet parts of my mind, not so little segments of pain made themselves at home. And there they stayed.

I hadn't talked to Avery since I'd moved out. We'd both upheld our no-contact agreement diligently. But then, on September 10th, I got a text.

"Hi Odette. Can we meet up? It's OK if you say no. Just want to talk."

It was an odd feeling seeing Avery's name pop up on my screen. He'd never left my mind, but the resolution of our relationship had imprinted more than the possibility of any sort of communication. We were, in every way, the past, not the present. But his message was like a flare summoning me to a familiar place. Avery had made a space for me, and perhaps because of nostalgia or loneliness or lingering affection, or maybe all three, I accepted it. I maybe even embraced it.

We met for lunch at a pizza place near our old – his – house. Oddly enough, despite the close proximity to where we'd lived for years, we'd never once eaten there. I couldn't decide what to wear for the occasion. Part of me, an old, dredged up part, wanted to impress him. Another part, the dominant one, wanted to be comfortable. I went with jeans and a tank top. Best of both worlds.

As soon as I saw him, I felt a rush of familiarity sweep over me.

Seeing him was like hearing the opening bars of an old favorite song for the first time in years. It was sweet and welcoming and almost exciting all over again. He'd asked to pick me up but I insisted on meeting him there. I had no idea what he was planning on saying. I wondered if maybe he wanted to discuss something logistical, like money he owed or I owed or some credit card in his name that I still had without realizing it. Something business. Something formal. But he didn't look formal when he stepped out of his car and walked over to mine just as I parked.

He was wearing a gray t-shirt and dark jeans. His hair was cut differently than it usually was – buzzed shorter on the sides than the top. It wasn't the Avery I was used to, but I liked it. He looked put together. He looked, in a way, happy. Peaceful. Like he'd fought a few wars in the time we'd been apart, and he'd won. I fought some battles too. But I didn't know then, as he reached for my hand to walk inside, if I'd come out on the winning side or the losing one.

I didn't take his hand. I didn't have much time to react to the offer of it before he took his back, perhaps embarrassed to have even made the gesture in the first place. We walked in side by side and seated ourselves. The restaurant was small and cozy, an intimate setting for an as yet unknown conversation. It was somewhat dimly lit, and the walls were covered with tacky posters of pizza places all over New York. The owner obviously had a fondness for hole in the wall joints, and it showed. It was quaint and charming, and made me feel a little bit more at ease. Avery led the way, picking a booth in the back that promised the most privacy. A middle-aged waiter with salt and pepper hair and tired eyes followed us almost immediately and gave us menus before hurriedly telling us he'd be back with waters. Everyone has a story and I stopped just for a moment to consider if he, too, had lost love, and his eyes still bore the weight of it. Regret is such a difficult thing to hide, no matter how hard we try. Our eyes always give us away.

I think that was the case with Avery, too. Only it wasn't regret I saw in his eyes as he looked at me from across the table. It was hope.

"Can I just get us a pizza?" he asked, his voice sounding rushed a little nervous.

"Sure. Whatever you want."

The waiter came back quickly and gave us two glasses of water before asking if we knew what we wanted to drink.

"Water is fine. Can we just get a large pizza with pepperoni, sausage, green peppers and mushrooms?"

The waiter seemed frenzied, having braced himself for a drink order and been thrust into our entrée choice. His mind was clearly occupied with other things, and memorization of orders was probably last on its list of priorities.

"Yes. Hold on. Sure. Be right back."

He left without writing anything down.

"Hope he got that," I laughed after he'd gone, trying to break the proverbial ice.

Avery laughed, a bit too loud and a hair too forced. He *was* nervous. My mind filled with little memories of his laugh, a sound I'd heard so many times and had so easily forgotten. And I thought of Parker's laugh. So different. My heart hurt looking at Avery. Because I missed him so much; I missed the beginning of us. And I missed the ending I never got with Parker. It's so odd to find yourself aching for two parts of two different stories, neither of which you'll ever see through, or again. I was eternally torn between wanting what was long since over, and wanting what could never be. Which is worse? Having something and losing it or knowing what you could have had and never getting to experience it?

"Is everything OK?" I asked.

"Yeah, everything's fine."

"I was surprised when you texted me. We haven't talked in a while."

"I know. I think separation was good, don't you?"

I did. But I wasn't ready to be done with it, not just yet. I needed more time. Time to think and grieve and reflect and move on. Time to figure out who I was without Avery and without Parker.

"I think so," I said.

He cleared his throat.

"I want to go out with you."

"What?"

"I want to take you out on a date."

"Avery."

"I know."

"We're divorced. We *just* got divorced."

"I know."

"So…"

"This time I've had, it made me think. And it made me realize that we gave up too easy. *I* gave up too easy."

"I don't know, Avery. I mean, we went to therapy. We did try. Maybe not as hard as we could have but we did try. And the issues we have…"

"I know," he said, cutting me off. "They're still there. I know that. And they won't go away. I hurt you and you hurt me and neither of us can change that."

My mind wandered to being with Parker in bed at home, the home Avery and I had, and I closed my eyes, trying desperately to shut out the thought of it – to forget just how badly I hurt Avery, even if he didn't know.

"I'm not saying we should get married again. Now or ever. I'm saying I want to be with you. I want to go out with you and spend time with you and start over, because what we had in the beginning was something, wasn't it?"

He was right. Our beginning was amazing. Our middle was hard, and our end was straight shit. But our beginning? That was book-worthy.

"Are you sure this is what you want?"

"It is. If it's what you want."

The waiter brought over the pizza on a small metal dish, one that looked far too small and far too weak to hold the monstrosity of a pie on top of it. I mumbled "thank you," and the waiter left quickly, as if he could sense the seriousness, and intimacy, of a moment in which he was unwelcome. I was grateful for his discretion. Avery and I both stared at the pizza, but neither of us touched it. It looked delicious, little bubbles of grease boiling on each slice, melted cheese running up through the crust. But I wasn't hungry, not in the slightest. I was just thinking. I hadn't even considered getting back with Avery. There was so much hurt and so much sadness, enough to fill ten lifetimes. But if we could go back to the beginning?

"You can't redo things, Avery," I said, answering my own question in my head out loud.

"I know. I'm not saying we can."

He paused and put a slice of pizza on his plate.

"I'm saying we start over. We're not redoing anything. We're not starting where we left off, or where we were 8 years ago. We're starting where we are right now. The Odette that's sitting in front of me right now, I want to get to know her."

In a weird way, what he said made sense. Not starting over, just starting.

"No pressure," he said. "Just hanging out."

He took a bite and chewed slowly.

"Do you want a slice?"

I nodded, even though I absolutely didn't, and took a piece, laying it carefully on my plate.

"Can I think about it?" I asked, sounding much more unsure than I would have liked.

"Absolutely. Take all the time you need. I'm in no hurry."

The way he said that struck me. He would wait for me. I knew he would.

I forced a smile. I had a lot of thinking to do, but at that moment, all I wanted was to think about anything else.

"Let's talk about something mindless," he said, as if he'd reached into my mind and pulled out the first wish he landed on.

"Yes. Please. Definitely."

He laughed.

"Like this pizza. Wow," he said, doing an exaggerated chef's kiss and taking a much larger bite than he should have.

I laughed. He always knew how to make me laugh. That hadn't

changed. Maybe it never would.

As the meal progressed, our conversation became less polite and more personal.

We talked. Actually talked. For three hours, we sat there, sharing details about everything we'd missed, not just over the past few months, but in the years we'd lost, even when we were together. But I didn't mention the station and he didn't ask. That part of my life, the work part, the Parker part, had to be separate. The conversation felt natural, as if we were two people with a spark of chemistry who happened to have shared history.

At the end, he asked if he could call me and, for a brief second, I felt almost like a teenager again.

"Yes, absolutely," I said.

He walked me to my car and opened the door for me, and then, politely and with the utmost respect, kissed me delicately on my cheek.

"Night, Odette," he said as he walked away.

I smiled and got in the car. I waited for him to drive away and then I just sat there with the engine running, thinking. I knew what I would say. I would say yes. And we'd start over and start fresh and start new and all of those burning cliches, and this time, it would probably work. Because I'd found what was meant for me and I'd lost it. So now there was nothing more to lose. Choosing Avery wasn't a choice at all, really. I felt like an explorer who'd strayed too far from home and stumbled on a beautiful, exquisite new place. I'd stayed there for a while, and I'd even felt like I belonged there. I'd built a little home and made it my own. But eventually, the place I'd found started to disappear. And I was left standing in a desert, holding onto a key that led nowhere, that opened nothing. So I went back home. Back where I belonged. You can long for happiness and accept contentedness all at the same time. You can want that place you had while accepting the one you have. Life isn't black and white. There are no nevers and no forevers. The world doesn't do well with absolutes. We exist entirely in the space between.

CHAPTER
TWENTY ONE

———————

Avery called me the next day, just like he promised. We set up some dates, once a week for the next month. Each one felt more natural than the last and, slowly, we fell into a comfortable routine. Seeing one another became normal again – even something I looked forward to. At work, Parker and I saw less and less of each other. We managed to avoid each other almost entirely some days, with the exception of shift activities like meals and training. Sometimes I would look over and catch him looking at me. I would smile and he'd give me a corny little wink, and his eyes would sparkle, and the split in my heart would break open just a tiny bit more. Seeing him was never not painful.

◆ ◆ ◆

On October 13, exactly four months since I'd moved onto Cedar St., Avery asked me to move back in with him. He didn't do it with any ceremony or romance. He just asked over dinner. He did it the way Avery would. Exactly the way I would have expected.

"I think you should move back in with me. I think we're ready," he said.

I looked at him, studying the lines and curves of his face. I loved Avery. I loved the way he felt things so deeply. I loved the way he cared about me, even if he didn't always show it. I loved him in a familiar way. I knew him. Choosing to be with him was like putting on an old sweater. It was comfortable. It was safe. Avery was my old home.

Before we left the restaurant, I told him I'd move back in with him at the end of the month when my lease was up. And I did. Two weeks later, I packed all of my things in a U-Haul and said goodbye to the little house that had been home for the past five months.

Everything about our old place looked the same. It was as if time had stood still while I was gone. Avery hadn't moved so much as a pillow on the couch. It was like his life stopped when I left and restarted when I returned. The past several months for us had been so different. I had experienced a whole lifetime while he waited and now, I was back again, ready to resume the life we had chosen together.

I always told Parker he played it safe. The truth is, so did I. I could've stayed on my own. I could've held out hope that something like the love I had with Parker could be found with someone else. I could've chosen to believe that someday, somehow, Parker and I would find our way back to one another. But I didn't. I chose what I knew. I chose Avery. I chose a life I could fall back on. I chose the love I knew over the love I wanted.

Life is full of landmarks, choices you make that define the rest of your days, however many you have. In the span of six months, I'd felt more love than I'd experienced in my entire life. And then it ended. And my world, the bubble that had expanded to encompass so much happiness I thought I never deserved, popped. And I landed back where I started. Almost as if it had all been a crazy dream.

Once, in one of our car chats, I pulled out my phone and read Parker my favorite poem -- "The Road Not Taken" by Robert Frost.

Two roads diverged in a yellow wood,
And sorry I could not travel both
And be one traveler, long I stood
And looked down one as far as I could
To where it bent in the undergrowth;

Then took the other, as just as fair,
And having perhaps the better claim,
Because it was grassy and wanted wear;
Though as for that the passing there
Had worn them really about the same,

And both that morning equally lay
In leaves no step had trodden black.
Oh, I kept the first for another day!
Yet knowing how way leads on to way,
I doubted if I should ever come back.

I shall be telling this with a sigh
Somewhere ages and ages hence:

Two roads diverged in a wood, and I—
I took the one less traveled by,
And that has made all the difference.

"What's it mean?" he asked when I finished reading.

"He had a choice," I said. "And he chose the riskier road. He chose to take a chance."

"Ah," he said, staring out the windshield. "Ol' Bob Frost. Making it all sound so easy."

I laughed.

"It is easy, if you make it easy," I said. "Everybody has choices. It's just a matter of what choice you make. Everything has risk, Parker. That's life."

He looked at me then, with those brilliant hazel eyes. He didn't say anything. He just looked. But I could tell what he was thinking. He was thinking that, if given the choice, he'd pick the safe road. He'd pick the road he knew. And when it came down to it, that's exactly what he did. And I guess, that's what I did, too.

Life is full of landmarks. Sometimes the people you choose don't choose you. And sometimes the life you settle for is enough because it has to be. Perfect love isn't meant to last and, sometimes, good love is good enough. I settled just like Parker settled. We chose, for different reasons, the life we knew over the life we wanted.

And that has made all the difference.

◆ ◆ ◆

Parker transferred at the beginning of November. He didn't tell me he was leaving; I found out from Daws when the assignments came out in October. There was a little party for him on his last day. He was off the week before, so I didn't see him until he came to grab the last of his things from his locker on the 30th. I was coming down the stairs as he was walking out, his denim jacket slung over one shoulder, duffel bag of forgotten odds and ends balanced on the other. He must've heard the door close behind me because he turned around briefly, smiled unevenly, as if his lips couldn't decide whether to part or not, and walked out through the open bay doors.

When I grabbed my gear, I felt a piece of paper in my coat pocket and pulled it out. It was from Parker, handwritten.

Odette, Lucy, Doll, Love…everything,

There's nothing to say that hasn't been said. And so I'll leave you with this. You once said Pablo Neruda was your favorite poet.

Here's something of his. I'd like to think I could say it better, but we both know I can't. So I'm letting him speak for me.

In another life, Lucy.

> *"But*
> *if each day,*
> *each hour,*
> *you feel that you are destined for me*
> *with implacable sweetness,*
> *if each day a flower*
> *climbs up to your lips to seek me,*
> *ah my love, ah my own,*
> *in me all that fire is repeated,*

in me nothing is extinguished or forgotten,
my love feeds on your love, beloved,
and as long as you live it will be in your arms
without leaving mine."

I pressed the note to my chest and closed my eyes, and embraced the little, painful dagger of closure that forced closed a door I'd never meant to open. A door that led me to that house in that land in that place that had been so much more than an escape. I'd held the key and now I could let it go. There was nothing left to open.

◆ ◆ ◆

Some people believe in love at first sight. I don't. I believe love is something that grows. It's not immediate, and it can't be forced. It comes as it pleases and leaves as it pleases, like the breeze on a spring day, or snow in winter. Or any of the other cliches people associate with transient things. Because that's just it: The feeling of love may be forever, but the act of it is a passing thing.

Everyone feels love in a different way. The word is just a general way of describing a complex emotion that hits us all in unique ways at unique times in unique situations. No love is ever the same. No two people feel love the same way, and no person feels love the same way twice. Love is a mixture of need and want, a four-letter lyric that generates no sound, yet creates the sweetest, most entrancing melody. It's all-encompassing and all-becoming, because when we're in it – when we're in this grand wave of emotion – we don't see anything else. We don't feel anything else.

Of all the things we as humans feel, love is the most confusing. It causes new pain and heals old wounds simultaneously. It opens scars inside us we never knew existed, while breaking open our hardest barriers and forcing us to be everything we ever dreamed for ourselves. It gives and it takes; it hardens and it softens. It is the most contradictory of emotions because it is, in itself, a contradiction. To feel love we must know the opposite of it. Love is innately rooted in fear. You cannot love what you wouldn't mind losing. What we love we cling to harder than a drowning man to that last, slowly breaking branch in the river. We want so badly for it to stay – knowing that nothing lasts forever – that we often-times force it away. We bat at it constantly, trying desperately to keep it in our clutches. But like that branch, it eventually breaks away and leaves us, destined for something else or someone else.

The act of love isn't meant to stay with us. But its shadow, the feeling of love, is always there. Long after the object of our affections has moved off, we still feel its grip. We still ache for that feeling. We yearn for the breadth and width of that love – the very love that ripped open our chests and tore the strings of our hearts to pieces. We want it because the pain is worth it. For most of us, one single moment of true, unadulterated love is worth years of turmoil. Knowing that there is this person on earth who looks at you and deems you worthy of that one sacred emotion not one of us can truly define is breathtaking and intoxicating. It makes us feel whole in a way we'd never felt before.

It makes us feel like we matter. Parker was right. Sometimes people aren't meant to stay in your life. Time is predictable -- we can always count on it to move us forward, even when we don't want it to. But I learned through all of this that people -- people are unpredictable. Some people you think will be temporary fixtures in your life end up becoming cornerstones in it. And others who you think will be around forever end up being as ephemeral as the changing seasons.

We give parts of ourselves to each person we love in this life, until little bits of us exist all throughout the world, contained inside some people who deserve it and some who don't. But knowing this, knowing that with each part we give we lose a piece of ourselves, we do it anyway, with reckless abandon. We do it because a few days, weeks, months or years of feeling that love is worth a lifetime of brokenness. We take that calculated risk and welcome its consequences because, as torturous as love can be, it can also be absolutely glorious to those who find it.

Sometimes, when I stop to think about Parker, when the memories creep back in from the recesses of my mind where I've locked them away, I feel the familiar ache in my heart that I knew so well when things ended between us. The piece I gave to him I can never get back. And, I do think, it was the most important one I had to give.

I don't expect we'll ever see each other again. But if we do, I think it will go something like this: We'll pass each other in a hallway or a crowded street. He'll be with his person; I'll be with mine. We'll look at each other only for a second. He'll smile and I'll smile but neither of us will stop, not even for a second. Because we'll know that our part in one another's story ended long ago. And my heart will ache and pull for him just like it did when we first parted, because though my story didn't start with him or end with him, it came alive because of him. And a heart doesn't forget something like that.